CRUEL *dynasty*

THE SINNERS SAGA

Beautiful Criminal

Beautiful Sinner

Beautiful Forever

THE DYNASTIES
BOOK TWO

CRUEL *dynasty*

GENEVA LEE

ESTATE
PUBLISHING + ENTERTAINMENT

To Josh,
Every book is for you

1

*"*N*o, you aren't, dirty girl. Kerrigan Belmond is."* The words played on repeat inside my brain like there was a glitch. Partly because I refused to process them, but mostly because I hadn't expected Holden to say that. I couldn't get it out of my head. Or any of the other questions it raised.

As I stepped back inside Sparrow Court, Iris caught me at the door, startling me from my heavy thoughts.

"What do you think about a fall wedding?" she asked, oblivious to my preoccupation. I actually liked Kerrigan's stepmother, unlike Kerrigan herself, who despised the woman for being closer in age to her than her father. I'd been taken back at first, but I'd discovered Iris was warm and kind. The former ballet dancer had an assured, calming presence that I envied—especially now.

"What?" I asked. Iris continued on, but I barely heard her. I caught snatches of what she was saying, but I was too distracted to worry about weddings or flowers or where to have the reception. None of those were my decisions to make anyway, a fact Holden had just pointed out.

My brain felt too full to even consider another question. The London residence of the powerful Byrd family suddenly felt more imposing than ever before. The large rooms meant to host lavish parties were relatively empty tonight save for the family and the Belmonds, my pretend family for the next eleven months. There was no distracting background noise or music. No crowd to lose myself in. The lack of people made the spaces feel like cavernous mouths opened wide to swallow me whole.

I forced a smile, looking around the living room for any sign of Spencer. Where had he gone? He'd called me into the house and disappeared. I had turned to leave when Holden, his twin brother, had delivered a bombshell:

"No, you aren't, dirty girl. Kerrigan Belmond is."

I'd laughed off his suggestion that I was an imposter posing as Kerrigan. But looking into his green eyes, all I found was certainty.

He knew the truth.

I had no idea how.

I had no idea what he would do about it.

All I had was questions. How long had Holden known? Was he going to tell his brother? But the one that rattled me the most: why did he call me out?

My gut told me it was a power play. A move meant to draw me away from Spencer and to him. I had no idea what he planned to do with the information, but I doubted he would stay silent long—unless I managed to convince him he was wrong. Or managed to convince him to keep my secret.

How far was I willing to go to keep him quiet? The answers that swam to mind were unsettling. Holden could get in the way of my arrangement with Tod Belmond. If he told Spencer the truth, the engagement would be off and I would have failed in my mission. If that happened, there wasn't a point to continue pretending. I couldn't let him talk, but I wasn't certain how to keep Holden quiet or what he expected in return for his silence. Maybe he'd hoped it would make me ignore Spencer and stay with him, even if only to pry information from him. My stomach twisted in a knot as I walked with Iris toward the sitting room. I'd made my answer clear by returning to Spencer tonight, but I knew that one decision wouldn't be the end of it.

I wasn't surprised that Holden might try to hurt me to make an impression. Although the brothers were identical in every way—and I'd seen enough of both to know—they were mirror images of each other. Duplicates and opposites at the same time. Whereas Spencer was reserved, his attention running the gamut between polite interest to considerate affection to bluntly sexual, Holden was the reverse. He was casually dismissive and flirtatious, the very icon of a wealthy, privileged playboy. But under that rakish veneer, I glimpsed his ability to manipulate people, as well as the vulnerability that drove his behavior. The brothers shared the same face and body but I'd only begun to peel back the layers to expose their differences.

"I'm sorry," I murmured when I realized Iris had paused to wait for my thoughts about something. "I think

Spencer was ready to leave, and I need to find him and tell Evie goodbye, and—"

"Oh, honey." Iris dropped an arm around my shoulder and gave me a sympathetic squeeze. "It was a big night. You've already made one decision, and, here I am, already planning the wedding. Go home with Spencer and get some rest." She winked at me as if to silently add *or do something else in bed*.

"Thanks. We can talk about it tomorrow or later." My vote was for later, but the longer I waited to get involved and slow down this runaway engagement, the farther my stepmother and his mother would get in making their plans.

In truth, I envied her excitement, because I wanted to plan a wedding and walk down the aisle and marry the man whose ring I wore. But that was completely out of the question. I wasn't Kerrigan Belmond. Spencer's brother was right. I was a stand-in for the London socialite meant to keep him—and everyone else—from learning the truth. Kerrigan had run away from her outwardly perfect life for reasons I was still trying to figure out. Her father had made it sound like she was merely acting out. When he'd been shown a photograph of me, he'd concocted a ridiculous plan to have me pose as his daughter until she finally came home. The most ridiculous part was what he offered me in return.

Ten million pounds.

It was an offer I couldn't refuse. But being Kerrigan had proved more dangerous than I'd anticipated, especially where my heart was concerned. I hadn't expected the feelings I had toward Spencer, the man Kerrigan was intended to marry, to burrow deeper than the physical attraction I'd felt at our first meeting. Now things with him were spinning out of control, particularly in the feelings department. And then there was his brother, who annoyed me as much as he intrigued me. I'd seen glimpses behind the mask he wore for the world, and I'd found myself tempted by him on more than one occasion. One night I'd even given into the temptation, allowing myself to be drawn into the brothers' twisted rivalry like a pawn. The result had been one of the most erotic experiences of my life, and one of the most shameful. Since then, I'd made my choice. It was easy enough given my agreement with Tod Belmond. I'd vowed to keep Spencer Byrd's attention. That should have been what made me choose him. It wasn't.

And that scared me.

Because this life wasn't mine. Neither brother was mine. I wasn't Kerrigan Belmond, and I never would be.

No matter how much I was beginning to wish otherwise.

I FOUND Spencer in the study, talking in low voices with his grandfather. Lord Byrd, the Duke of Wellesley, was one of the most powerful men in the House of Lords and one of the few who still held a peerage. His gray head was bent in contemplation, listening to the discussion. My body tightened as it swept over Spencer. The tailored suit that he'd worn to dinner this evening only reinforced his broad shoulders and the lean, muscular body that waited for me underneath his clothes. His effect on me was dizzying, even when he didn't know I was in the room. Maybe that was why after waiting my whole life to lose my virginity, I'd given it to a man I was being paid to entertain. It was an expectation of the arrangement, but I hadn't gone to bed with Spencer because of that. I hadn't been able to stop myself. At his touch, I came alive. He'd promised me pleasure in his bed, and then he had shown me that he kept promises.

Tod Belmond, Kerrigan's father and the only person here who knew the truth about who I was and why I was here, stood with them, listening. I paused at the door, straining to hear what they were saying, and hoping I didn't get caught eavesdropping. The longer I spent around Tod, the more convinced I was that he was lying. But about what? I suspected that the key lay somewhere in his agreement with Lord Byrd—that Spencer and Kerrigan should marry—but what did Tod hope to gain? He claimed he wanted to take care of his daughter and see her rise in London society. But his story was beginning to fray at the edges. I'd found Kerrigan's computer in a bag in his office. I'd been given her ID. She'd left nearly everything behind, and increasingly, I was beginning to wonder if she'd taken anything at all. *Or* if she was ever returning. I couldn't shake the feeling that she wasn't off sunning herself in the South of France as the story went. She was in danger— serious danger.

And not only was I one of the few people who knew that, playing my part well meant no one would help her. Not if they thought I was Kerrigan—alive, well, and happily betrothed.

Since Tod had returned from the countryside with Iris, he'd been watching me more closely. I had expected him to be happy that Spencer had proposed. Thanks to me, he was one step closer to bridging the two families. But he seemed more wary than jubilant. Tod had celebrated the announcement like everyone else, but he'd spent the last few hours watching me at the dinner table. His eyes followed me whenever we were near each other. Had he figured out that I had broken into his office while he was away on holiday? Did he know that things between me and the Byrds were more complicated behind closed doors than I'd let on? Was he concerned that I might be attempting to steal Spencer for myself?

I couldn't blame him for thinking that. Ten million pounds was a life-changing sum of money. It would help me escape my past and start over. But the truth was that it paled in comparison to what I stood to gain by becoming Spencer Byrd's wife. He had to wonder if that was my plan now.

I knew that because I'd begun to consider it myself.

Kerrigan didn't want to come back. Or maybe she *couldn't* come back. My body went cold at the thought as if it sensed that the woman whom I resemble so closely—that I had fooled nearly everyone, but Holden, into believing I was—was herself as cold as ice. I shuddered to think what that meant.

I didn't know how to find her. I wasn't even sure I wanted to, but watching the men plot and plan, I realized I might be the only one who could. I cleared my throat, knocking softly on the door to let them know they had company. "Sorry to interrupt, but I need my fiancé to take me home."

I reinforced this lie by yawning widely.

"Of course," Tod said, not bothering to even look in my direction. "I will speak to you later...unless you'll be staying at Spencer's flat this evening."

Heat flooded my cheeks. It was strange how comfortable Tod was sending his daughter to Spencer's bed. Then again, I wasn't his daughter. Maybe he had an easier time remembering that than I did. "Oh. Um, we haven't discussed..."

"It's fine," Tod cut me off. He gave the men a knowing smile as if to say that he knew we were leaving for reasons other than my exhaustion. But when he turned it toward me, it stopped at his eyes. They remained hard and wary, glinting like obsidian in the dim light of the office. I was a solution that was turning into a problem, because ten million pounds wasn't enough to turn off my brain. He didn't trust me. I didn't think he particularly liked me.

That suited me just fine because as he stared me down, I felt the truth in my bones.

Tod Belmond knew where Kerrigan was hiding and why she had run away.

Because he was the reason she was gone.

2

____

"**Y**ou're quiet," Spencer said as we started down the drive. He paused the car at the gates, waiting for them to open, but when they did, he didn't pull forward. He was waiting for me, but I didn't know what to say.

"Holden," I muttered, hoping this was enough of an explanation to explain my malaise.

Spencer's hands tightened on the steering wheel at the mention of his brother's name. After a moment, he loosened them, but his face remained a stony mask. "Do you want to come home with me or go to your house?"

"Neither," I said flatly, then quickly added, "I want to be with you, but not if..."

"Yeah, I know." Spencer understood why I didn't want to return to the flat he shared with his brother in London proper. "I'm beginning to think it's time for me to move. This is bollocks. I loved that place."

"We could make him move," I suggested. Instantly, a

wave of guilt hit me. Was I really going to come between them? Especially knowing that in the long run I had no claim to Spencer, his ring, or his heart?

Spencer shook his head. He was still rigid, sitting ramrod straight in his seat. A muscle tensed in his jaw as he stared at the road ahead. He didn't speak for a few minutes. We passed the turn off to Willoughby Place, and soon I realized we were on our way toward the heart of London. I didn't ask where he was headed until he drove toward Westminster—the opposite direction of his flat.

"I assume there's a plan," I said softly.

"We need to find our own place," he bit out. My chest tightened as if to contain the heart that had just skipped a beat inside it.

There was no point getting attached to the idea of Spencer and a home. Tod Belmond would never agree to let me live elsewhere. And I couldn't risk putting down roots. It was too dangerous. Under the guise of being Kerrigan, I was safe for the moment. That couldn't last forever. I forced a pitiful laugh. "I don't think we'll find a new flat at this hour."

"Not tonight." He actually smiled, and the mood in the car lightened. Now instead of feeling like we were trapped in invisible quicksand, I only felt like we'd been caught in mud. It was a negligible improvement. "Tonight, we are staying elsewhere."

"Where?" I looked out the window for clues as to where we were headed. London whizzed past in a blur of lights and motion. Like most major cities, it never slept entirely. Eventually the traffic would lighten and shops would close. But despite the late hour, London was still brimming with life. A few of the bigger stores were still open, ready to welcome late-night shoppers, and nearly every pub was serving the late-nighters and would be for a few hours still.

Construction signs rerouted us, forcing us to pass by the Palace of Westminster, Parliament, and the cluster of tourist traps that had grown like weeds amongst the important buildings. Crowds of people swarmed the sidewalks as we drove across Westminster bridge. Nearby on the banks of the Thames, the London Eye spun lazily. The McLaren shot past the sights with decisive speed and didn't slow until Spencer pulled to the valet parking spot in front of the Westminster Royal hotel.

I stared up at the impressive building, which rose into the night sky with a sense of its own prestige. This wasn't the kind of place I was used to going when I needed a spot to crash. In fact, I'd never been in an actual hotel, let alone a five-star hotel in one of London's most expensive areas. I was still gawking when the valet opened my door.

"Welcome to the Westminster Royal, Miss," he said as he helped me out of my seat. "Do you have any baggage?"

"No," Spencer cut him off, already around the car and by my side. He stretched out his hand, the keys to the McLaren in his palm "I'm afraid this is a last minute trip."

The valet hesitated at the offering. "I should warn you that the hotel is near capacity."

If this concerned Spencer, he showed no sign of it. Instead, he buttoned his suit jacket, then offered me his arm. "I'm certain something can be arranged."

Spencer bypassed the front desk where a man was angrily demanding an adjustment to his bill and went straight to the concierge. She smiled up at him from behind her stand. Her glasses reflected the screen of her computer and she pushed them higher on her nose.

"May I help you?" she asked.

"Serina," he said, reading her gold plated name tag. "I need a room, preferably the penthouse suite, and some items delivered to it as soon as possible."

She chewed her lower lip, glancing toward the front desk. "I don't actually handle rooms."

It was a testament to the authority that radiated off him that she wasn't laughing at his request. Instead, she seemed to be nervously figuring out how to help instead.

"But you can get someone who can. Please tell the manager on duty that Spencer Byrd needs to speak with them."

The size of her eyes doubled as she recognized the name. Bobbing her head, she chirped, "Let me find him."

I couldn't help staring at the people coming and going from the lobby as we waited. I'd been around rich people since I came to London as Kerrigan, but for the first time I felt a perceptible shift in how I felt. After the initial thrill of stepping inside the extravagant hotel, I'd been surprised at how ordinary everyone looked. I forced myself to study them harder. They weren't ordinary at all. They weren't like me. They were like Kerrigan. A woman lingering near the entrance to the attached bar wore a fur cape around her shoulders despite the sultry summer evening. A few men wearing tuxedos talked animatedly near the elegant sofas in the lounge. Clearly, they had just come from some kind of event. Everywhere I looked there were small hints at the fabulous and luxurious lives the people staying here lived. From diamonds dripping down necks to Louis Vuitton trunks being wheeled toward the lifts, I was in Kerrigan's world, not mine. But for the first time, I found myself oddly comfortable about it.

I suspected that had to do with the man at my side and not any change within me. I was still Kate. A shitty waitress. Alone in the world. Desperate to get away from my own mistakes.

Serina returned with a man in a blue-pinstriped suit. His blonde hair was gelled neatly at the sides and dark eyes studied us with interest that bordered on contempt.

"Mr. Byrd, Serina tells me that you're looking for a suite this evening," he said in an American accent that caught me off guard. He didn't like being called to deal with a customer, and perhaps, owing to his being American, Spencer's name didn't hold the same gravitas it had with the concierge. "This is peak season for the Westminster Royal, so naturally we are completely booked. We have a party arriving—"

"Who are you?" Spencer cut him off.

The young man flinched, visibly annoyed, but kept his composure. "I'm Cyrus Eaton, the new manager."

My eyes darted to a brochure waiting in a gilded holder on the concierge's podium. They were turned to the side to keep from falling, which helped me read the logo printed at the bottom of the paper.

An Eaton Hotel.

So much for my time in a five-star hotel. If he was an owner and he was unwilling to help us then we probably needed to look elsewhere. I tugged at Spencer's arm. "We can find somewhere else."

"The car is already in valet," Spencer said, not budging. He turned back to Cyrus, who was waiting for a reply still. "I'd like to speak to Lord Eaton."

There was something undeniably hot about the confidence he exuded as he spoke. Spencer walked as if he owned the world. But he wasn't dealing with a desk clerk, he was dealing with someone who had to be very high up in the ranks here. That didn't phase him one bit.

"My grandfather has retired for the evening," Cyrus said. "Perhaps, if you come back tom—"

"He'll want to speak with me tonight," Spencer interrupted. He leveled a meaningful glance at Cyrus, who looked torn between continuing their pissing contest and giving in to the request.

Something sparked in his dark eyes and then cooled, finally he agreed. "I will call up to him. If he is unavailable—"

"He won't be." Spencer shoved his hands in his pockets.

Cyrus Eaton strode away, taking his time and pausing at the desk as he went. He was sending a message that while he would do Spencer's bidding, he was still in charge. If only he could prove it. Spencer snorted as the manager finally disappeared into his private office.

"What a little man." Disdain oozed through his words.

Did he think that because Cyrus had condescended to

him or because Cyrus had acquiesced? I couldn't say. "Do you stay here often?"

"No. There's not a point, since I have my flat," he said casually.

Of course, Spencer didn't need to stay in a hotel when he lived nearby. We were here because of me. No, we were here because of Holden.

"However, my grandfather knows Lord Eaton. If that wanker is who I think, his grandfather will promptly put him in place." He drew a deep breath and shifted to face me. "What do you need for the evening?"

"You," I answered instinctively.

"Done." His lips twitched and he bent to give me an appreciative kiss. "I rather meant personal care items. A favorite toothpaste? Lotion? Face cream? Nightgown? I want you to be as comfortable as you would be at your own home."

"That's not necessary." I shook my head. "I'm sure they have things I can use in the room."

"They won't be what you usually use. That's not a problem?" He seemed genuinely surprised at how little I seemed to care.

"It's not," I said, "but—"

"Mr. Byrd!" We both turned at the call of his name. Cyrus was walking swiftly toward us wearing a tight smile. "I apologize for the misunderstanding. I didn't realize. Well, it hardly matters. We've arranged the Presidential Suite. It will be ready in a few minutes. In the meantime, Serina will assist you with whatever else you need."

I swallowed back a smile at the sudden, and obviously uncomfortable, shift in his attitude toward us.

"Thank you." Spencer barely acknowledged him more than this. Instead, he looked at me. "Why don't you have a drink in the bar while I see to the rest of the arrangements. I'll join you in a moment."

I glanced over my shoulder, looking for the bar. Cyrus came to my aid.

"Allow me to show you inside and get you a table."

There was backpedaling, and there was grovelling. This was the latter. He crooked his arm. Next to me, Spencer cleared his throat and Cyrus's arm dropped to his side. Message received.

"This way," he said tightly.

The hotel's attached bar was dimly lit by a few overhead lights, stationed over the marble-countered bar. Behind the counter, two bartenders busily prepared cocktails with the ease and efficiency of machines. The rest of the space had no overhead lights but at every table a candle flickered under a glass dome, casting each in a romantic glow. Other than some soft background music, the only sound filling the place was a low roar of murmurs and whispers. How many people were having affairs here? First dates? Anniversaries? Everywhere I looked, posh couples sat with their heads bowed together in intimate conversation.

Cyrus showed me to a table in the corner, far away from the bar. "What can I order you?"

I started to say that it was unnecessary and I would wait for Spencer, but then I remembered the part I needed to play. I doubted they had any wine labels I knew of. In fact, I didn't really have a signature drink as it were. Instead, I blurted out the first one to come to mind. "Martini."

"Dirty?" Cyrus asked.

I had no idea what that meant, so I nodded. Wasn't dirty always better? The drink arrived around the same time as Spencer.

"Can I get you something to drink?" the bartender asked as he placed my glass in front of me.

Spencer studied my choice momentarily then nodded at it. "The same."

"Very good." The bartender bowed his head and then returned to mix the cocktail.

"May I?" He plucked the stir stick out of my martini. "I'm starving."

With a flash of his perfect white teeth, he tugged an olive into his mouth. Was it possible to be jealous of a fruit or vegetable or whatever the hell an olive is? Because I was. My thoughts drifted to places I wanted to feel his teeth.

"That's a dangerous look," he rasped. "What are you thinking about?"

"Just wishing I was that olive." I picked up my glass and took my first sip. I blinked, my eyes watering at its strength. I took another, pleased that it went down more smoothly. I hadn't known what to expect, but I actually discovered that I liked it.

"That's funny." His eyes sparkled as he spoke, the candle's flame dancing in them. "I was thinking the same thing."

The bartender delivered his drink and we sat in silence for a moment. I stirred my drink, distracted by thoughts of Spencer and annoyed by thoughts of Holden. I found myself wishing that I'd been told more about the Byrds. It would have been nice to know I was dealing with two men instead of one. Increasingly, I understood that was the case. Whatever Holden thought he knew, I needed to find out. That left me very much under his thumb. I had to tread carefully if I didn't want Spencer to find out. I wasn't positive Spencer would even believe his brother, but it wasn't a risk I was willing to take.

"You're quiet again." Frustration rippled through his words. "What did Holden say to you?"

I hated that he knew exactly what pressed on my mind, because it would only serve to fuel Spencer's rivalry with his twin. But neither of them showed any signs of wanting to give up their secret feud. That left me stuck in the middle of them. Maybe I could have escaped it before that night in their flat. Now I couldn't pretend that Holden's advances were entirely unwelcome. I'd given them what they wanted, realizing too late that in actuality, I'd taken what I pleased instead of the reverse. Even worse, I wondered if I'd be able to resist that temptation again.

"Nothing, really. He was just toying with me. I don't think he's pleased about the engagement." All of that was true as well as obvious. I wasn't telling Spencer anything he didn't know. I was just leaving out the bombshell that Holden had dropped on me at the end of the evening.

"Of course he isn't. He wants you." He sat back in his seat with a heavy sigh. One hand raked through his hair, disheveling it and reminding me of how it looked after we made love. My thighs squeezed more tightly together as though someone might be able to hear my clit pounding nearby. But his next words stopped it. "I thought if he had a taste, he would drop it."

"A taste?" I'd written our near ménage à trois off as a drunken mistake, but now I saw what it truly was: a calculated gamble.

"Kerrigan." Spencer's voice dropped so low that it tickled on my skin. "I told you before that we shared other women. It wasn't out of the question for either of us to think..."

"And what about what I thought?" I asked coldly.

Spencer looked away, the telltale muscle in his jaw tightening. He was holding something back. I was beginning to learn his ticks.

"Out with it," I murmured, and his eyes flashed to me in confusion. "Whatever you aren't saying, just say it. I promise not to run."

"You enjoyed it." The words were half accusation and half reminder. "I felt how wet you were. Tell me the truth, how far would you have gone with both of us?"

I swallowed, knowing no answer could erase the truth of the matter. That was why he had taken me so roughly that night. He needed reassurance that I belonged to him—that I was his to enjoy and no one else's. But there was one thing he couldn't see.

"As far as you wanted me to," I replied in a clipped tone. Picking up the martini, I downed it in a single gulp. "You don't seem to understand, Spencer. I'm yours to do with as you please. You wanted me to suck off your brother and you wanted to watch. So, *tell me the truth*, how far did you want to take it?"

The shadows in his eyes darkened, and he opened his mouth. "You want the truth, Kerrigan?"

My mouth went dry, but I nodded.

"I would have—"

Before he could finish his sentence, a smiling Cyrus Eaton—the world's worst hotel manager—interrupted. "Your suite is ready. Please let me know if you need anything else this evening."

Staring into Spencer's eyes, I wondered if I might need a ride home. Not to Hampstead, but to West Bexby. I hadn't left much there. I'd never had a lot to begin with, but I was starting to question if any of this was worth the price it would exact in the end. Was ten million pounds worth my soul?

3

One of the many perks of the Westminster Royal was private lifts available only to their most important guests. The drawback was that there was no one else to distract you if you were in the middle of an uncomfortable disagreement with your fiancé. Spencer had barely looked at me as we made our way to the upper floors of the hotel. I had expected him to return to the topic we'd been discussing when the hotel manager interrupted us, but he seemed to be studiously avoiding it—and me.

The lift deposited us on a private floor with only one door. Spencer unlocked it and pushed it open, stepping to the side to let me pass.

I took one step into the room and gasped. It was practically a flat. In actuality, it was likely bigger than most flats in London. Floor-to-ceiling windows made up the outer walls. Sheer curtains had been drawn to reveal glimpses of the city below. There was a sitting area meant for entertainment and a small bar where a bottle of champagne was chilling in ice. Spencer crossed to it and picked up a note placed beside the bucket. He read it, snorted, and tossed it back on the counter.

"It seems Mr. Eaton is quite apologetic over his behavior earlier," he explained to me when I arched an eyebrow.

I nodded, still struck temporarily mute by my surroundings. Every time I thought I was used to the insane world of the rich and the famous that I'd found myself in, I was surprised. There was a sense of dominance standing here, kilometers above the city, watching the tiny lights of cars and life below. No wonder businessmen always wanted the penthouse suite. It had to do a lot to fuel the ego. I wandered to the window and watched the London Eye turn for a moment, mesmerized by the way its lights reflected on the dark surface of the Thames.

"You act like you've never been in a hotel room before," Spencer noted a curious strain of surprise in his voice.

"It's the view," I lied. "I don't usually stay in the city." Another slip-up and this one he'd nearly caught. Kerrigan wouldn't be impressed with this view. Not given the life she lived. I had to find a way to curb my shock when I found myself in unpredictable situations. The question was how?

"Why would you with your house so nearby?" He bought my cover-up easily. Spencer stripped off his jacket, tossing it over a nearby chair. "I'm going to order room service. What do you want?"

"I'm fine." Any lingering hunger I'd felt had vanished at the bar. A twisting sense of nausea replaced it.

"You barely ate dinner tonight." His words were blunt, lacking the concern that might have seemed inherent to the observation.

"Excitement," I murmured. I pressed my hand to the glass, marveling at how I could blot out the individual lights below with the tips of my fingers.

"What's your excuse now?" he growled.

I closed my eyes, searching for the right words, and decided there were none. Spinning around, I slumped against the window. He was standing in the shadows, making it hard to see his face. Somehow that made it easier to be truthful. "I feel sick."

"Because of our fight," he guessed, his temper cooling a little.

Was it a fight? It hardly felt like enough to be called that, but why else would it have had this strong of an effect on me? I supposed that meant it was, so I nodded. "I can stop wondering what you were about to say." I cleared my throat, nerves bubbling inside me. "I asked you how far you would have let things go."

Spencer didn't move from where he stood, so I couldn't see his reaction to bringing this topic up again. There was a long pause, and I began to wish I'd left the subject with the empty martini glasses at the table.

"All the way," he finally said softly. The dangerous edge had left his voice, making his words sound hollow. Not because he didn't mean them, but because he wished he didn't. "I would have let Holden fuck you. Part of me still would."

A lump of tears formed in my throat, and I swallowed

but it did nothing to dissipate the heat. I didn't know why this bothered me so much. I'd been turned on when he'd hinted at his darker desires regarding sharing my body with Holden. The night I'd been with both of them, I'd been the one to encourage the encounter. I'd egged them both on, taking the role of temptress willingly. Even now, arousal ticked inside me, betraying that I couldn't deny I was attracted to both men.

"Do you even know why?" I asked after a moment. "Why do you two do that?"

"I think it would take a panel of psychiatrists to decide that." He finally took a step out of the shadows and crossed to the sofa. Dropping onto it, he leaned forward burying his face in his hands.

"It's more than sex. If it was only that, you wouldn't have..." I trailed off, worried that I was pushing things too far. Spencer was right. The brothers might need therapy, but I was hardly qualified to give it.

"What? What did I do?" He didn't look up at me. His face remained in his palms.

"After it happened..." I gulped, praying I wasn't making a mistake, and plunged forward. "The way you touched me that night. It was like you needed to prove I belonged to you. I felt like you were claiming me."

He finally peeked up through his fingers and sighed. "I was."

"That's the problem. If it was just about pleasure, I don't think we'd be having this conversation. We might have had a hard time looking at each other over breakfast, but we wouldn't be fighting." If it could just be physical, things would be different.

"That's what you wanted." He sank into the back of the sofa, a gloomy expression on his face. "You wanted pleasure, and we dragged you into our fucked up game."

"I shouldn't have—"

"You did nothing wrong, Kerrigan," he cut me off. "Holden kissed you. I led you to believe I wanted to share you with him."

"And you didn't," I added.

"I did. I didn't." He shook his head. "Fuck, it's not black and white. Can't you see that? It's why I need to keep you away from him."

I realized then that Spencer wasn't afraid of losing me to Holden. He was afraid that he'd give in to their game and regret it. Memories of that night flashed through me, turning my core molten, as I recalled how it had felt to have my lips wrapped around Holden while Spencer pleasured me. I would have taken things farther that night. Part of me regretted holding back. In that moment, I hadn't known what would happen after or how either brother would respond. I'd lost my only chance at being claimed by both of them. I couldn't risk encouraging any more temptation where they were concerned. I wasn't strong enough to resist. And I wasn't certain Spencer or Holden were either.

"We've shared everything," Spencer continued, "but he's a stranger to me. When we were kids...it's hard to explain."

As I listened to him struggle for words, I knew I had to make a decision. I took a deep breath and hoped I wasn't choosing the wrong path. "Your grandfather made you compete against one another."

Spencer lifted his head, confusion churning in his eyes. "How...?"

"Holden told me when he drove me home that morning," I confessed. "He said that you were forced to become rivals to see which one of you would be the better heir."

"And I won," Spencer said grimly. "I suppose it's better that way. Holden doesn't want anything more than to fuck around with every pretty thing he sees."

I hesitated, unsure whether to confess any more of what Holden had told me. It was one thing to admit that I knew why their relationship was strained. It was another to betray the choices Holden had made in an attempt to protect his brother. That was for him to reveal. But keeping quiet, left me in the difficult position of trying to help Spencer see what had happened from a different perspective.

"I think that's why he wants you so badly. That and..."

"And?" I prompted. The more I understood what drove Holden, the better equipped I would be to deal with his flirtations. It would also help me ensure I could keep him from telling anyone else about his theory that I wasn't who I claimed to be.

"He's falling in love with you," Spencer muttered, his gaze focused intensely on the window.

I laughed, unable to contain myself. "Holden is too in love with himself to fall for anyone else."

"I know my brother." Spencer's voice remained as flat

and lifeless as his eyes. "He wants you. I can't blame him for that. I don't even deserve to be the one who gets you."

A weight lifted from my shoulders at his words, and I finally realized how keyed up I had been since my own confrontation with Holden earlier this evening. In its place I found sadness. I hated to see them being torn apart, and I wished there was something I could do to bring them together. But getting involved with both of them could only lead to disaster. We'd only narrowly avoided it before.

So, Spencer had admitted his twisted desires. Now that the initial shock had worn off, I knew we needed to find our way back to each other. Crossing the room, I dropped to my knees in front of him, a task made slightly more difficult by the fitted skirt I was wearing. I gripped his thighs, angling my head to catch his eyes, but he remained in the shadows.

"I belong to you," I whispered. "I promised you that when I agreed to wear your ring. Whatever happens, we'll get through it together." I ignored the pang of longing that stabbed me as I made a vow I wouldn't be the one to keep. I could only hope Kerrigan would come to see that Spencer was worth the fight.

"I bought you in exchange for a title and a bank account," he said miserably. "You barely know me."

"I don't know everything about you," I admitted. "But I want to. That's what we agreed, right? Tell me, if it wasn't me, would you be free to marry anyone else you chose?"

"No."

"The same for me." I knew somehow that was the case. If it hadn't been him, Kerrigan would have been traded like a commodity to another wealthy, important man. She was an asset in her father's portfolio. While part of me believed Tod Belmond loved his daughter, the other half wondered if he knew how to love any other way. Did any of these people know better?

He finally dropped his hands, the hint of a grin playing on his handsome face. "Are you saying that we could do worse?"

"I guess," I teased, relaxing a little to hear him crack a joke. "Actually, I think we're lucky. I think we could be happy."

It was the truth. I believed Spencer could make Kerrigan happy. I believed that he wanted a real marriage. Why else would he have demanded we—or rather they—forego a prenup? Why did he care so much about bringing me to climax as much as possible? He was still keeping distance between us as if waiting for something to go wrong, but he'd shown repeatedly that he wanted me.

He wants her, the voice in my head reminded me, *and you will never be her.*

"What was that?" Spencer asked.

I shook my head, freeing myself from my conscience. "What?"

"You flinched like you were in pain. Are you okay?"

"Nothing. I was just thinking about dealing with Holden." It was an easy lie to reach for, but I regretted it when his eyes darkened.

"We can't get away from him no matter how hard we try," he grumbled. Spencer shoved his hand through his hair and glanced toward the side table, avoiding my eyes. Bringing up Holden had returned him to the gloomy state he'd been in when we first arrived. We'd taken two steps forward and three back. Would it always be like this? "I should order room service. You're hungry."

Part of my job, if it could be called that, was to keep Spencer happy. I told myself that I needed to do something because of that, but the truth was more complicated. An acidic taste coated my tongue as I realized that I didn't want to soothe him because of the arrangement. I just wanted to see him smile—like he had the night he'd finally proposed. Things hadn't felt so dire that day. Actually, we'd both been almost giddy since—until tonight. Until the party.

Weren't parties supposed to be fun? All I felt was a vague and frustrating sense of duty to attend, and this was the second time I'd left a group gathering wishing I'd never gone at all.

I needed to do something to change the mood.

"You're quiet," he noted and my gaze fluttered back to him.

I pushed a smile onto my lips as I reached a hand behind my back. It was dark enough in the suite that Spencer couldn't see what I was up to. That gave me the element of surprise, which I was certain I needed if I was going to get his mind off his brother.

"I was just thinking...that I am hungry." I dropped my voice into a silky murmur that seemed to ooze across the room. "But not for food." I had already unzipped my dress to the small of my back. Now I slipped it off my shoulders and allowed it to puddle at my feet.

He shifted in his seat, throwing his arms over the back

of the chair, and relaxed. His gaze burned into me as I dropped to one knee, then the other. Leaning forward, I planted my palms on the ground. Spencer's hand found his crotch and he adjusted himself as I moved on all fours toward him. It felt deliciously dirty to crawl, breasts swaying and my naked sex exposed to the air. When I reached his feet, I waited for a moment. Somehow, I knew that was what he wanted—what he expected. He shifted, reaching down to grip my chin and tilt my face up. "What are you hungry for?"

I nuzzled my face against his hand as I sat back on my knees. But when I reached for his belt, he caught my wrist with his other hand.

"I asked you what you're hungry for," he repeated himself.

"You," I murmured, my eyelashes fluttering to the floor. I wasn't sure what I'd done wrong, but it must have been something because he didn't release me.

"Open your eyes," he said gruffly, his eyes boring into mine. I wanted to look away, but I couldn't. His hand was still on my chin. "Tell me exactly what you want."

I flushed, excitement and embarrassment fighting for control of my thoughts. "Your...cock."

"That wasn't very convincing." He released me and relaxed into the chair again. "Try again—and Kerrigan—ask nicely."

So that was how he wanted to play it. I might have been annoyed by his game, if each second that I kneeled, naked, before him, wasn't turning me on more and more. Spencer didn't bother to look away. Instead, they skated over me, drinking in my flesh, fucking me with his eyes until I could feel myself getting slicker and hotter.

"Please, may I have your cock?" I whispered, but there was nothing timid about the request. Instead, I pressed my face to the inside of his trouser, kissing his thigh through the fabric. "Please give me your cock." I continued kissing, moving my body to nestle between his wide-open legs. "I want to taste you...I want to taste your cock."

He raised an eyebrow.

"Please," I added quickly.

"Since you're being so polite." He loosened his belt. It fell open and he proceeded to unzip his pants. I licked my lower lip as he pulled his dick out. He'd started to harden already, but I knew that his already generous organ would get harder and longer—and I wanted every inch of it. But when I bent to take it in my mouth he held up a finger. Adjusting his pants, he freed his balls. He smiled as he issued a one word command: "Lick."

I'd told him I was hungry for him and it seemed he wanted me to prove it. I'd given him a blow job before, but I'd already lost count of the number of times he'd crept between my thighs to put his mouth on me. Spencer devoured me like he'd been starving his whole life. It was so intense that I often lost my handle on conscious thought. All I knew was that his mouth was claiming me.

I wanted him to feel the same way now.

Dipping my head, I brushed my tongue over his balls before drawing it up his shaft. He wanted me to lick and I wanted to please him. It was an urge that was becoming almost instinctual. I swirled and flicked, earning a grunt of approval that swelled in my chest. Spencer's fingers caught the hair knotted at my neck and yanked my face up.

"I don't want a blowjob," he rasped. I blinked in confusion, but before I could shift up and offer whatever part of me he did want, he continued, "I want to fuck your mouth. Would you like that?"

Oh my. The gush of arousal between my legs would have answered for me if he could feel it. I bobbed my head as much as his firm grip would allow me to move. He tskked once and I realized my mistake.

"Please fuck my mouth." I stared up at him, waiting for him to take what I offered.

Spencer brushed his thumb down my cheek. "So perfect," he murmured. "Such a lady on my arm, and when you're on your knees? You're every fantasy I've ever had."

I swallowed as unexpected emotions swirled through me. Spencer tugged me backward, giving himself room to stand. When he was on his feet, he urged me up until I was face-to-face with his groin. "Open your mouth, beautiful."

My lips widened into a large O and he brought the tip of his cock to my mouth. He guided it in slowly, and I relaxed, welcoming the intrusion.

Spencer groaned as he slid the final bit, pushing himself deep into my throat. "I don't know how the fuck you do that, but christ, it's hot." He shifted a bit and I fought the urge to gag. I'd never let a man be in control like this before, but for some reason, I wanted nothing more than to let him use me.

"I love seeing you there, swallowing my cock. I'm going to fuck your mouth now. Ready?" The tenderness in his voice was at odds with the primal control he held over me. Somehow that made it even sexier.

I bobbed my head as far as I could without choking, and Spencer smirked. "It's not fair to ask questions you can't answer. If you want me to stop, just pinch me. Okay?" He shook his head. "I did it again."

I placed a hand on his wrist and rubbed a circle on it. His eyes hooded with understanding and he rocked against me slowly as if testing the waters. I kept myself still and open, even as my eyes burned from the effort. It only made me want him more as he moved faster, thrusting harder and harder. At that moment, I wasn't Kate or Kerrigan. I'd become pure sensation, desire drenched every inch of my body. I only wanted him and the sweet oblivion he offered.

I would take whatever he would give me so long as I was here with him. Spencer went rigid and I accepted his climax. When he finally stilled, he released his grip on my hair and coaxed me to my feet. My knees wobbled as I stood and when his mouth closed over mine, capturing my tongue, I swayed dangerously. His hands sank into my hips, keeping me steady until finally he broke away. He didn't speak as he swept me into his arms and carried me to the next room.

There was nothing gentle when he dropped me onto the bed. Before my body had settled against the mattress, Spencer sank to his knees, pushing my thighs apart. And then he devoured me.

4

I stared at the white gown, torn between picturing myself in it and wanting to throw up. My fingers tightened around the champagne flute in my hand, a complimentary gesture meant to showcase the celebratory nature of trying on wedding gowns. I glanced at the price tag, hanging from a delicate silk ribbon and took a large drink. Maybe I was wrong and the champagne was meant to lubricate the sale. I couldn't imagine how much alcohol I would need before I would consider spending that much on a dress to wear one day.

But I wasn't paying. Tod Belmond was, because it wasn't my wedding dress but his daughter's. Price was no object—a fact he'd made clear when he sent Iris and I off to the bridal salon this morning. I'd had a slight stomach ache ever since.

Christina, the stylist who'd fawned over us since we stepped through the door, sauntered over, her lips beginning to form a question. Then they took a sudden downward turn. She snagged the tag and tucked it quickly into the bodice.

"I'm sorry you had to see that." She pressed a hand to her chest, looking as though I'd just witnessed a murder. "It was terribly crass. I'll speak to the girl who pulled that dress."

"Oh, don't." I shook my head, which made me feel a little tipsy. I swayed on my feet but managed to recover without her noticing. "It doesn't bother me at all. It's just money."

That's what Kerrigan would say, or what she would think, at least. Maybe Kerrigan would be offended to see the price tag hanging so blatantly off the gown. I was starting to understand that the only thing rich people liked more than spending money was spending money with blind abandon. Nothing proved how rich they were more than that.

"More champagne?" Christina asked.

I looked at my empty glass. I wanted to say yes. "No. I skipped breakfast. It's probably not a good idea."

"I understand," she whispered. "The dress diet. Every bride I know stops eating the moment he slides the ring on her finger."

I pushed a smile onto my lips, my brain fighting me the whole way, and nodded. That was a perfectly normal, albeit insane, excuse for missing breakfast. I'm sure most brides did go on a diet. But I wasn't most brides. In fact, I wasn't a bride at all. I'd skipped breakfast, because I'd run out of time.

When Iris had arranged the appointment after we'd

announced our engagement to our families, a month had seemed like a long time to find a way to get out of dress shopping. At first, I'd ignored the problem, because it only reminded me that I was playing dress up with another woman's fiancé. Then, I'd allowed myself to be distracted by playing other games with Spencer. It was easy to forget that the clock was ticking when I was in his bed. Soon, I'd forgotten entirely until Giles had reminded me of the appointment when he brought me my morning coffee.

Now I was standing in a dress shop, surrounded by tulle and lace and silk, and all the complicated emotions I'd avoided for the last few weeks were churning in my stomach along with that glass of champagne.

"Do you have one you'd like to try first?" she asked.

I shrugged, resisting the urge to look toward the dress I'd spotted the moment we'd walked into the private salon. The perfect dress. The dress I would choose to walk down the aisle to become Spencer's wife.

The dress I wanted but would never wear. "I'll let you choose."

"Shall we step into the changing room to get your measurements and—"

"Can I speak with my assistant for one moment before?" I cut her off.

"Of course, I'll bring some gowns into the room and we can get started when you're ready." She bustled off just as I felt a familiar blackness creeping along my brain.

"No, no, no," I murmured, looking around wildly for Giles. I lurched forward when I spotted him near the window. He was so absorbed with something on his mobile, he didn't see me.

Each step toward him became harder, the dark edge of panic pulling against me and trying to drag me down. I was struggling to breathe when he finally looked up, realized what was going on, and caught me mid-collapse.

"What on earth..?" He gripped my elbows, supporting my weight and I blinked rapidly, trying to keep myself from passing out. "You need to sit down."

Giles led me to a chair, casting a furtive look over his shoulder, to see if anyone had noticed the incident. Iris had paused in the adjoining showroom to look at dresses for herself until we called her in to start the fitting. Christina had been occupied. Thankfully, no one but Giles seemed to have witnessed the spell.

"I knew this would happen," he announced. Standing, he swiped his glasses from his face and wiped them down, his expression shifting from surprise to concern. "I told you that you needed to eat something this morning."

"It was just a panic attack, not low blood sugar," I grumbled, feeling better now that I was off my feet. I relaxed into the comfortable, oversized chair.

His head tilted, studying me like an owl. "Has this happened before?"

"Yes, sometimes it happened before," I admitted. There'd never been enough money in my life before. I'd been a shitty waitress, and I had no family to rely on to help me. I was well-acquainted with panic. Anxiety was my oldest friend.

"And recently?" he pressed.

"A couple of times." *A day*. I left that part out. "Don't worry. I have it under control."

"I can see that," he said dryly. "I'll make you a doctor's appointment."

"No," I blurted out, dropping my voice quickly. "Won't the doctor know that I'm not…I mean, we probably have different blood types or something, at least!"

"Our personal physician is very discreet. I'm certain Tod would want you to speak with him, and I can assure you that anything you tell him will be kept private."

"Thanks, but it's unnecessary. I think you're right, actually. It was probably champagne on an empty stomach. I'll be fine."

"I think—" Before he could badger me further, Iris fluttered into the room. She spotted us and the smile fell from her face.

"What's wrong?" she cried, rushing toward me.

"Champagne on an empty stomach," I lied again. Next to me, Giles glowered but he didn't say anything. Somehow I doubted this conversation was over.

"Oh darling, should we reschedule? This heat probably isn't helping if you're not feeling well." Iris bit her lower-lip. It was painted the exact shade of plum of the toes showing in a pair of leather slides. Her white, linen shirt dress draped elegantly over her slender figure. It was a far more casual look than she normally wore, but London was unusually warm for mid-September.

This was the out I'd been looking for, practically served

to me on a silver platter. All I had to do was say yes and I'd buy myself more time. But how much? A few days? Weeks? Until Kerrigan arrived and reclaimed her life, I was her stand-in, even when it came to moments like this. "Maybe just some water?"

"I'll get it," Iris said, adding, "and I'll check to see if they have air conditioning. I can't wait for autumn to get her ass here already."

Air conditioning was a long shot, but given the price tag on that dress, maybe we would luck out.

As soon as she was out of earshot, I turned a wild look on Giles. "I can't do this."

"What?" he said.

"This." I pointed around us. "I can't pick out a wedding dress."

"You'll be fine," he said, his tone taking on an effect I liked to think of as *soothing Giles*. "I'll guide you."

But he couldn't soothe me now. "You don't understand. I can't pick out *her* wedding dress."

He stilled as though he hadn't expected this. When he finally spoke, his voice was strained. "Does it bother you to try them on?"

"It's not my place to pick out another woman's wedding dress. What if she hates it?" I hissed. But that was far from the real reason I didn't want to do it. Not only did it feel wrong, but there was something worse than that.

I hated the thought of picking out a dress for her to wear. I hated the idea of trying on a perfect gown, of hearing how beautiful I looked, of picturing Spencer's face when he finally saw the dress I'd chosen. All because that moment belonged to her. It wasn't my place to choose just like it wasn't my place to get attached to Kerrigan or her world. Picking out a dress for her to wear as she finalized her happy ending didn't feel like a burden. It felt like a punishment.

Half an hour later, I'd been measured, strapped, tucked, and trussed into an extravagant embroidered gown that weighed approximately an imperial ton. It took two of the shop attendants to help me out of the dressing room and into the salon. Iris gasped when she saw it, but Giles merely pursed his lips.

"The embroidery is hand-sewn and contains approximately one hundred thousand Swarovski crystals," Christina explained.

That explained the price. I stood awkwardly in front of two full length mirrors. Kerrigan stared back at me. This was her world, not mine. Seeing myself in the wedding gown reminded me of that.

"You look stunning!" Iris got to her feet and moved to study the dress more closely. "What do you think?"

I met Giles' eyes and he imperceptibly shook his head. Apparently, Kerrigan wasn't a glutton for punishment either. I hoped that meant trying on less extreme gowns.

"It's a bit much," I said, not wanting to offend Christina regarding her choice. It was a beautiful gown, even I couldn't disagree with that. The heavy silk had a silverish hue complemented by an intricate, intersecting pattern of beads and crystals that undoubtedly contributed to its weight. The 3 meter long train probably didn't help. The dress itself rose high on the neck, which although elegant, felt claustrophobic, especially in the warm salon. And given the hundreds of tiny buttons that ran from the back of my neck to the end of the train, it had taken an eternity to put on. I'd need a small army to help me dress the day of my wedding.

Kerrigan would need a small army on the day of her wedding, I corrected myself.

"I think you're right. Although you look lovely," Iris said. She turned to Christina with a warm smile. "Maybe something less..."

"Heavy," I jumped in, earning a laugh. Even Giles smiled.

The next gown fit that bill and was much more comfortable. Long lace sleeves wrapped delicately down my arms, the lace continuing across the bodice, which stopped just below the bust and flowed down in a cascade of chiffon. It was delicate and airy, easy to move in and elegant. I looked at Giles as I made my way —without anyone's help — into the salon. Iris lit up again but he snorted.

"People will assume you're pregnant if you wear that," he said matter-of-factly.

Iris shot him a scathing look. "Who cares? People already assume that. What matters is if she likes it!"

She turned expectantly toward me, but I was too busy trying to rehinge my jaw. Pregnant?

"People think I'm pregnant," I stammered, trying to process this information. "Why would people think that?"

"Everyone assumes that with short courtships," Giles answered for her. "The rumor mill never stops churning."

"My 'bump' was all over the tabloids when we eloped," Iris said with a sympathetic smile, but real pain glimmered in her eyes. "They didn't give up until no baby arrived. If there's no scandal, the press can always cook one up."

My hand instinctively pressed to my stomach and I grimaced. I couldn't imagine having stories like that written about me. "So no empire waists?"

"I'd steer clear of them," Giles advised coolly. "Besides, this doesn't really say Kerrigan Belmond-Byrd to me."

"Are you hyphenating?" Iris asked as if to seize on a less painful topic.

"I don't know," I admitted with a sigh. "I need to think about it." I wondered how often I would be using that line in the coming weeks. I wanted to avoid any decisions that might have long-term repercussions for Kerrigan when she returned. I ignored the tiny voice that whispered *if* in my head.

She would come back and marry Spencer and I would move on and finally be in control of my life.

I tried on a few more dresses, but none met Giles' silent approval.

With each rejected selection, Christina's smile grew

more strained. When she followed me into the dressing room to help me out of the last gown she'd pulled for me to try, she seemed on the verge of tears.

"I have one last dress for you to try on," she said, and I swallowed a groan.

I waited for her, stripped down to the restrictive corset I'd been stuffed into for this ruse. At least, in underwear, the woman staring back at me felt like me. I slumped onto a tufted stool and reminded myself that it was almost over. I'd even managed to successfully avoid choosing a dress. I doubted I'd be allowed to resist forever, but that would give me time to grill Giles for what Kerrigan would want in a dress.

"Last one." Christina chirped as she entered carefully carrying a gown. The moment I saw the golden shimmer of its fabric, my heart splintered.

It was the dress. The one I'd spotted when we arrived. The one I'd been grateful to *not* find in the dressing room. It was the dress I would choose to walk down the aisle.

It wasn't Kerrigan's wedding gown. It was mine.

"Just give it a chance," she said, misreading my expression. "I know it's not the most traditional in terms of the fabric, but it's fit for a fairytale."

I answered with a tight smile, unable to speak as she helped me into the gown. Like some of the others, it required help from an assistant due to the number of buttons. But I didn't care. Each one they fastened only made the dress feel more right.

And that was all wrong.

The gown's fabric was embedded with thousands of

tiny crystals, so small that it did little to add to its weight. From the front the dress was a simple, elegant choice. Its bateau-like neckline ran across my collar bone and ended with two artful lace appliques that wrapped over the shoulder. The delicate, glimmering fabric then extended down the arms, stopping just below the elbow, and fastening there with a row of buttons. The natural, precisely tailored waistline would leave no room for speculation about baby bumps, and the skirt swished and swirled around me as I turned to admire it in the mirror. The fabric caught the light and practically glowed. But it was the unexpected back of the gown that had caught my eye. From the front the gown was modest, behind it took on an edge of sensuality that was still sophisticated. Lace framed the sheer fabric that ran from my shoulders to the small of my back, interrupted only by a row of those delicate buttons. She'd been right. I felt like a princess.

But the story I'd wandered into wasn't mine.

"There," Christina said, smoothing out the train. When she stood, she grinned widely. "Do you love it? I don't know why I didn't pull it before."

"It's..." I tried to say fine or okay or something noncommittal but the words lodged in my throat, unwilling to come out. Not when words like spectacular and brilliant and gorgeous existed.

"Let's show your friends," she suggested.

I didn't correct her use of friends. I was too overwhelmed to find any words at all.

As I stepped into the salon, the total silence that fell in the room told me what I already knew. I'd found the dress. I fought the urge to cry, even as heat pricked my eyes. It was a stupid reason to be upset. I'd never have spent that kind of money on a dress. No fairy tale wedding awaited me. But if the world was perfect, and far less cruel, this was what I would wear down the aisle to say my vows. What were the chances that my dress would be the same as Kerrigan's?

"It's perfect," Iris said, voicing my thoughts. Giles could only nod, taking my final hope with it. If he had disapproved, I had an excuse to walk away.

A throat cleared behind me, sending my heart fluttering as I recognized the familiar sound. I whirled around, sending the skirt swirling like a sea of stars around me. My breath caught as my eyes met his green ones.

A muscle ticked in his jaw as our gazes locked. Inside my chest, my heart swelled, a reaction that was becoming dangerously routine to Spencer's presence these days. I found myself unable to speak as we stared at one another. We didn't have to. I could see everything he was thinking reflected in the emerald pools of his irises. The dirty thoughts came first, and I could almost picture how he would lift the skirt to take me, unable to wait until the wedding night to consummate our union. But that greedy desire quickly cooled into something more intense—something that felt dangerously like actual love. I saw it on his face. I felt it in my bones. I was in way over my head, and this time it wasn't a panic attack that left me drowning.

I blurted out the first thing that came to mind. "You can't see me!"

"I can't..." He repeated the words, confusion taking hold of his handsome face. He flinched for a moment, looking away, and when he turned back, a cocky smirk had replaced the intense longing he'd worn only a moment before. "Still can't tell us apart, huh?"

Holden. Of course, it was Holden. I mean, why wouldn't my fiancé's twin brother show up at my gown fitting? I huffed and lifted the dress, suddenly eager to get out of it and everything it stood for. "What are you doing here?"

"Mother sent me," Holden said, sounding as frustrated as I felt. "She wanted to be here, after all, but she's stuck in Seychelles, and, clearly, Spencer can't come. So she sent me."

I doubted anyone ever felt stuck in Seychelles. I'd been thrilled to discover she'd be unavailable to dress shop, although I'd been sad to hear Evie would be with her on holiday. Trust her to find a way to make the situation unpleasant even eight thousand kilometers away.

"She also wanted to know as soon as you've chosen...the dress." The word sounded oddly thick on his tongue.

"I think we just did," Iris said brightly, either oblivious to the tension hanging between Holden and I.

"Yes, indeed," Giles said, getting on board, even as he watched the two of us warily. "It's a beautiful choice, Kerrigan."

Tears clawed up my throat, leaving a raw ache in their wake, but I refused to give in and let them see me cry—let him see me cry. Because he knew the truth. I still didn't know how. I'd avoided him as much to please Spencer as to protect myself. Now I was certain I'd been right before. I was being punished and Holden had been sent to deliver the final blow.

It took every ounce of determination I had to lift my shoulders and let them fall in a disinterested shrug. "Maybe."

I didn't wait for them to argue as I turned and headed back to the fitting room with Christina at my heels. She began to talk about the fitting schedule and what my options were in terms of veils.

"I'm sorry, but this isn't the dress," I cut her off. I couldn't bear the thought of it being her dress. I'd find something else. "I'm certain we'll find the right one next time."

"Next time?" she repeated in disbelief. "Let's not pretend you'll be back here. This is the perfect dress, so if you don't want this one, you need to go somewhere else. You're running out of time."

"There's tons of time. I'm sure that the next collection—"

"I don't think you understand," she interrupted me. "You have a week, maybe two, to order a gown in time for a December wedding."

I stared at her before a laugh burst out of me, finally erasing the tears I'd been holding inside me. "If that's what you're worried about, don't be. I'm not getting married until next summer. Plenty of time, see?"

"That's not..." she paused, confusion clouding her face. "I confirmed the date with your assistant this morning. It's right here."

She turned her clipboard to show me the notes she'd

been collecting throughout the day. I ignored the comment she scrawled that mentioned I was both indecisive and demanding and skimmed to the note marked 'date of wedding.'

December 18th.

I stared at the crisp, neat handwriting as though it might morph into a different day.

Just three months away.

Not nearly a year like Tod had said when he asked me to fake being his daughter. I told myself he must have had word from her. That was the only reason he would have asked Giles to give this date. Kerrigan must be coming home sooner than expected. Because the only thing worse than spending the day playing pretend and choosing Kerrigan's wedding dress was being expected to wear it as I took her wedding vows.

"I think you chose a beautiful dress," Iris said as we rode back home an hour later. "It's stunning and unusual—just like you."

The acid churning in my stomach made it difficult to smile, but I managed. It wasn't her fault that I'd been caught off guard. We'd wrapped things up at the bridal salon in time for afternoon tea, but I had asked to skip the reservation we'd made at the nearby Orangery. I didn't think I could stomach a single thing, especially not another moment of pretending I was fine. Giles had found a convenient excuse to duck out of the bridal salon before I could confront him about the date the shopgirl had been given. He wouldn't be able to avoid me forever. But even if he'd known—and not warned me—he was only the messenger, and it was poor form to shoot the messenger. I might strangle the messenger though. Just a little.

Nope, there was only one person that owed me an explanation. I'd been planning my attack since I'd begrudgingly ordered the gown for Kerrigan's wedding. Tod Belmond was going to tell me exactly what was going on tonight. I wouldn't allow him to keep any more secrets from me. He was the one who had talked me into his insane plan, but boundaries needed to be set.

I crossed my ankles staring down at the pair of Valentino sandals I'd chosen from the closet this morning. Delicate straps crossed each other adorned with golden studs. I'd learned the hard way that brushing one of the studs against my skin hurt. The shoes were beautiful but dangerous—just like everything else in Kerrigan's life.

"You've been very quiet since we left the shop. Is everything okay?" She paused for a moment as if gathering up some courage. "Does it have something to do with Holden?"

"Holden?" I laughed despite how angry I felt. "Why would it have anything to do with him?"

"I saw how you two looked at each other when he showed up," she said carefully.

A surge of adrenaline shot through me, leaving me both hot and annoyed. I tapped the arm rest between us, shaking my head. "I thought he was Spencer."

"I saw how you two looked at each other *after* you cleared that up. I know it's none of my business—"

"You're right, it isn't," I snapped.

Iris flinched at the sharpness of my words and guilt smothered the anger smoldering inside me. "I'm sorry. If you ever want to talk..."

"He's flirted with me," I said wearily. "It upsets Spencer for obvious reasons, and there was this moment."

Part of me wanted to tell her desperately. I hadn't even owned up to the night I'd spent with the two of them the last time I'd spoken to Eliza. But I hadn't. Partially because I'd felt ashamed, but partially because I couldn't admit that I'd liked it—to her or anyone.

"Moment?" Iris prompted with a raised eyebrow.

"I kissed him. Holden, I mean," I added quickly. "Another case of mistaken identity."

Iris's mouth formed a surprised O-shape. "Does Spencer know?"

"Oh, he knows. He saw." I slumped against the leather seat as my thoughts warred with each other. She didn't need to know more than that. It was enough to admit something had happened, right?

"And he overreacted?" she guessed.

"That's the thing. He didn't. I guess it's happened before." I was clearly in fibbing territory now, but there was some truth to it. Spencer hadn't minded. It had happened before. The part I was leaving out was that he had encouraged it, and the trouble was that was what I needed to talk about the most. "I guess they've, even, um..."

"What?" Iris asked innocently.

"You know..." I searched for a word that wasn't too loaded. "Shared before."

"Shared?" she repeated like it was new to her. Then, her brown eyes widened as her mouth fell open. She shut it with a hasty, "Oh!"

"Yeah." I closed my eyes, torn between relief and embarrassment.

Silence fell between us and I wished I hadn't brought it

up. I just needed someone to talk to about it. Spencer couldn't be trusted to give an objective point of view on the matter. I suspected Holden would say anything to serve his own agenda. Part of me thought Eliza might be the right person to discuss it, but she'd been working doubles and I hardly needed to bother her with my champagne problems.

Iris finally broke the silence. "Do you think they want to do that with you?"

"Yes. No. I don't know." I hung my head.

"Actually," Iris said thoughtfully, "that was the wrong question. Do you want to do that?"

This time it was my mouth that fell open. I blinked a few times to make sure I wasn't dreaming. There was no way that she had just asked me if I wanted to have a three-some with the man I was arranged to marry and his twin brother.

"I mean, the chemistry between you and Spencer is undeniable," she continued. "And Holden is identical to him. It's not exactly a hardship to allow two handsome men to take you to bed."

"Oh my god." I wished a hole would open and swallow the car.

"Sorry. I'm being nosey."

"No, I just..." There were so many things that Iris didn't know. Some of them she could never know. But there wasn't an ounce of judgment in her questions. It was like she knew I needed to talk. The trick was talking without giving too much away. "I was a virgin when I met Spencer."

"And now you're not," she guessed, a smile playing on her lips. "But you don't have a lot of experience."

"I don't really know about any of these things," I admitted. "I mean, how would you even…" I caught myself before I could finish the thought, blushing furiously.

"Judging from what you said, they could show you." She didn't bother to hide her grin now.

I buried my face in my hands. It was so hot I thought I might actually have caught on fire.

"I'm sorry," Iris said softly. "I shouldn't tease. There's lots of ways it could work, but only if you want it to happen."

I peeked up at her. "I think it would be a bad idea."

"Why?"

"They're too competitive. I already feel like I'm caught in a game between them. I don't want to cause more problems. Besides, it's wrong, isn't it?"

"As long as you're doing what you want with whomever you want, there's nothing wrong about it. But if you think it's going to cause problems then you should consider if the price is too high." Iris covered my hand with hers and squeezed. "Follow your heart. It will know what to do."

I wanted to tell her that my heart wasn't the one likely to get me into trouble. It was the trollop between my legs causing all these problems. But the truth was even more complicated. How could I follow my heart when it wasn't my life these decisions could affect?

The car pulled up to the gates, pausing for them to open, and I smiled gratefully at her. "Thank you."

"For what? I don't think I was very helpful." She laughed, shouldering her purse as the car pulled into the circular driveway to the front entrance.

"For not thinking less of me," I said quietly. "You know, for even thinking about..."

"Women give up so many things for house and home and husband and children. A woman should never feel guilty for taking something for herself, especially pleasure. Men owe us that much."

"I guess they do," I mused as the driver opened my door. I stared up at the estate. I wouldn't feel guilty for having desire just like I wouldn't feel guilty for taking control of my life, even if it was only a little control. Iris might have been talking about my relationship, but she'd hit upon something more far reaching than romance. No matter what I'd promised Tod Belmond, this was still my life. I deserved to know what was going on, and I wouldn't wait a moment longer to find out.

We made our way inside as the staff brought in our purchases. I'd consoled myself after being forced to order the perfect gown for my wedding ruse by buying every scrap of lingerie the boutique offered. Iris had gotten in on the fun, as she'd called it, and I did my best to ignore exactly whom she planned to wear the scanty underthings for. But while I looked forward to seeing Spencer's reaction when he saw some of the items I'd purchased, which ranged from bridal innocence to kinky vixen, it had done nothing to squash the anxiety burgeoning inside me.

"Do you want to have a cup of tea?" Iris asked, shedding the Philip Treacy hat she'd worn to the appointment. She passed it to a waiting maid.

"I think I'd like to change and have a few moments to myself," I said with a hint of apology.

But as usual, Iris understood. "Of course. I'll have the kitchen bring up a tray for you. If you do want to talk more, just let me know. I'm never far."

I nodded, a lump sitting in my throat. Iris was too kind. It made me feel guilty for keeping Tod's plan from her, and I'd begun to worry about what would happen when the real Kerrigan returned home. I'd been told that she didn't like her young stepmother. The more I built a relationship with Iris, the worse it would hurt her when she found out the truth. And I'd begun to realize that she would have to be told. Still, I couldn't stand the thought of being here when she found out the truth. She'd been so kind and I'd lied to her every moment. But I also didn't know how I would have managed even the one month of my arrangement that has passed without her.

A sudden swell of emotions propelled me forward and I caught her in a hug. "Thank you."

"For what?" Iris sounded surprised and amused but she returned my embrace warmly.

"For being here." I knew all too well that people didn't always show up in life. I'd lived most of my life alone until this point. The days of counting Iris as family might be numbered but I'd cherish each and everyone of them.

GILES WAS WAITING in my bedroom. He looked as though he was bracing for a storm with his shoulders squared and his chin raised. I blew past him, refusing to meet his eye. I didn't speak until I heard the suite's door close behind me.

"You might have warned me," I grumbled as I tossed

my clutch on the bed. The pale pink Valentino held little more than my mobile and a few credit cards, but it perfectly matched the sandals I'd chosen right down to the golden studs. I'd been clutching it so hard that they'd left tiny imprints on my palm.

"I was only informed this morning that your father, excuse me, *Mr. Belmond* and Lord Byrd had made a decision regarding the date," he said in a clipped tone, following me into the bedroom.

"I want to talk to him as soon as I change out of these sodding shoes." I yanked one sandal off and threw it towards the closet. It hit the wall and slid to the ground.

"Unfortunately, Mr. Belmond has been called to business in the city," Giles explained.

I finally looked up at him, zeroing in on the twist of his lips. He knew he was the messenger and that I wanted blood, and judging from his pained expression he didn't blame me. "Of course. How convenient."

"Indeed," Giles agreed. He cleared his throat, continuing on more tentatively than normal, "There is a more pressing matter."

"More pressing than me actually getting married as Kerrigan in three months?" I asked.

"For now, yes." He tilted his head slowly as if afraid that one wrong move might detonate me. "You have guests."

7

Giles had briefed me on the way down, but I didn't feel prepared as I stepped foot into the drawing room to greet Kerrigan's guest. I'd managed to get away with small talk when cornered by her old school friends at parties, but this was entirely different. Beatrice Highclere wasn't simply a schoolmate of Kerrigan, the two had been roommates at Woldingham and gotten into all sorts of trouble, according to Giles. The only saving grace—and the hope I clung to like a life preserver—was that there had been a falling out before university and the two hadn't spoken for years. He hadn't prepared me for how comfortable she seemed around Spencer, whom she was talking animatedly with on the couch.

The two barely looked up as I entered the room. Beatrice laughed, her hand extending to brush Spencer's arm lightly. His answering grin made my stomach sink. They knew each other *well*. It was obvious, and it made me feel nauseous. A cold chill crept over my body as I considered what I did know. Beatrice had attended St. Andrew's alongside both Spencer and Holden. Whatever hope I'd had that they hadn't known one another dissipated with each second that passed leaving only icy certainty in its wake.

Beatrice might have been Kerrigan's friend once, but she'd also clearly been close with Spencer. The question was how close?

I coughed lightly to interrupt the intimate scene unfolding in front of me. Spencer turned to me, his grin turning into a full-blown smile that thawed me considerably. He was dressed for the warm, fall weather in a button down shirt, its top button unfastened casually, and well-cut charcoal-grey trousers. My eyes skimmed over the slight bulge near his groin, wondering exactly how excited he'd been by his reunion with Beatrice.

"Kerrigan!" Beatrice called shrilly, clasping her hands together but not bothering to stand. She was the picture of propriety in a loose garden dress that nipped in at the waist but otherwise draped romantically around her svelte figure. Honey blonde curls were captured loosely below her ear in an elegant twist that was both informal and chic. She looked as though she might easily go from a garden party to a tennis match to an afternoon tea with little effort to reimagine her wardrobe. I, on the other hand, had changed quickly from the dress suit I'd worn to the bridal salon into a cream silk shell that I'd tucked into a high-waisted pleated skirt that stopped at my calves. The tall wedges I'd paired with it took the outfit from boring to sophisticated. I'd left my hair down, opting for nothing more than a pair of Kerrigan's large diamond earrings and the oversized engagement ring on my left hand.

"Bea," I said with a forced smile, using the nickname Giles had given me during our too-brief overview of Kerrigan's relationship with her. "What a lovely surprise."

Beatrice raised a plucked eyebrow, studying me for a moment. "Is it? I wasn't certain it would be."

Her question stopped me in my tracks. Despite knowing about their falling out, Giles had no idea what had caused the rift between the two friends. That left me at a serious disadvantage. I could only hope that offering honey rather than vinegar would garner more answers. "It is. The past is in the past."

Her cornflower-blue eyes slid to the man standing between us before she answered, "I'm glad to hear that. It was such a silly row in the first place, and it looks as though it hasn't changed anything."

I didn't miss the biting edge of her words—or how she looked at Spencer. I fought another wave of nausea. It hadn't simply been a fight that came between Kerrigan and her old friend. It was clear that Spencer played into it somehow. But how? Kerrigan had barely known Spencer, having only met him as a child. Of course, according to Tod Belmond, the arrangement of their marriage had been in the works since they were infants. Kerrigan couldn't have staked a claim on her future husband before they'd really met, could she?

I already knew the answer to that question. I'd seen it myself. These wealthy family dynasties didn't merely own land and houses and cars, they owned people. I was proof of that. I'd allowed myself to be bought and sold by the Belmonds. If Kerrigan believed that Spencer belonged to her, she very well could have punished her former friend for showing interest in him. Even now, I felt jealous at the thought that he might share a past with the beautiful blonde.

"And what was the fight about?" Spencer asked as he stepped toward me. He circled an arm around my waist and drew me closer to him. Given that we had company, he didn't greet me with the usual kiss, but despite its absence, I felt him marking his territory.

"A boy," Beatrice said in a coy tone. "Isn't it always?"

"Should I be jealous?" Spencer asked me.

I stared up at him, my whole being ensnared by his mere presence. For a moment, there was no one else in the room but him. "No."

"I hear congratulations are in order," Beatrice called, breaking the spell he'd cast over me. "Have you set a date?"

"*We haven't,*" I said tightly, "but it seems our families want a Christmas wedding."

Spencer's eyebrow shot up, and a burden lifted from my shoulders. I hadn't been sure if he'd known about the December wedding date, but he seemed as surprised as I was at this news. "Is that so?"

"Maybe my father and your grandfather should get married instead," I grumbled. "They seem far too interested in wedding plans for old men."

"I'll make sure to mention that to him," Spencer said dryly. "Oh well, it hardly matters, does it? We made our decision. They can obsess over the spectacle."

I had no doubt that spectacle would be the right word for it. I kept this thought to myself and decided to bring the matter up with Spencer again when we were alone. I needed to know how he really felt.

"Then there's no reason for you to stay in London at the moment." Beatrice smiled widely. "I told you it would work out, Spencer."

"You did," he said, a slight strain to his voice. "Still, it's hardly the summer."

"Parliament isn't back in session for weeks. Surely, your grandfather can't object to you spending time with your fiancée while he's on break."

"What's this about?" I cut in, feeling as though I'd wandered into a discussion mid-way through.

"Beatrice is attempting to coax us out to Yorkshire for a fortnight. Some type of impromptu reunion."

"I'd rather stay longer," Beatrice continued on for him. "Yorkshire is so lovely in early autumn. I always feel as though I've wandered into a Brontë novel, don't you?"

I was surprised to see she was looking at me. I'd never stepped foot in Yorkshire before, at any time of the year, but she couldn't know that, so I simply nodded. Beatrice's eyes narrowed for a second before she returned to her entreaty.

"And poor Edward needs us. He's back from America, and I hear he's still avoiding London," she explained. "Poor boy. I hear he can't even talk about darling David."

Pieces began to fall into place, and I stifled a surprised gasp as Spencer spoke, "I doubt a prince is in serious need of companions."

"He could probably use some friends," Beatrice retorted. "I hear through the grapevine that things are worse at the palace than they've let on. Can you even imagine?"

Given the near constant stream of tabloid fodder the royal family produced, it was hard to picture more drama behind closed doors. I'd never placed much stock in the latest gossip surrounding the king and his family, but according to their own statements, they'd endured a rough year. Edward had lost his husband under mysterious circumstances and that hadn't been the most shocking revelation they'd shared with the public. Still, I found myself siding with Spencer. If Edward wanted to be alone, he should be left to live peacefully. "Has he asked you to join him?"

Beatrice snorted, lifting her slight shoulder in a shrug. "Good friends know what you need when you don't know what you want."

"I just..." I searched for a way to get out of this trip. Even if Beatrice and Kerrigan hadn't spoken for years, it would be too difficult to keep the truth from her.

"I actually think it's a brilliant idea," Spencer said, catching me off guard. "Hensley House is vacant. The tourist season is over, so we don't have to worry about a barrage of unwanted ticket holders. I could use a break from London, and it sounds like you might like to avoid wedding planning."

"It's not that bad," I hedged. "It was just a long day and your mother sent Holden to the appointment—"

"Holden was there?" Spencer went rigid, his entire body locking up, as though I'd triggered his defenses.

"He came by to deliver a message. Your mother can't keep her opinions to herself, even from Seychelles."

"Two more good reasons to head north. I received word from my mother that she was coming home earlier today. I suppose you aren't the only one who just found out that the date was set," he explained.

I hated to admit he was right, but knowing that Caroline Byrd was returning to London changed the equation a little. Maybe I could get by for a few days with Beatrice.

"I've already informed Welbatten that I'm coming, and I'm trying to reach the old crowd." Beatrice spoke directly to Spencer with a familiarity that squeezed me with each word. Perhaps, she was one of Kerrigan's oldest friends, but she'd clearly been close to Spencer. "I think it's exactly what Edward needs." She rose from the seat, smoothing down her chiffon skirt before moving toward me. "I really am glad to see you, Kerrigan, and I do hope we can move on now that things are settled for you."

"Of course," I murmured, not trusting myself to speak too loudly.

"You really should come. I'd love to catch up." She leaned forward and brushed a kiss on both of my cheeks. "Cheers!"

I didn't turn to watch her say goodbye to Spencer. Something told me it would only make my decision harder.

"We don't have to go," Spencer said roughly as soon as we were alone.

I sighed, tipping my head back to gather my thoughts. "We won't be at the same house."

"Of course not. We'll be at Hensley and she'll be at Welbatten," he said, as though he couldn't imagine sharing his country estate with anyone. Somehow I doubted that size was the issue at hand, but I didn't press the matter. "Why? Do you want to keep me to yourself?"

Spencer shifted, turning my body against his. I molded against him and tilted my face up to his. "Would that be terrible?"

"Not at all. I don't really know Edward all that well," he admitted. "Seems like a nice guy. His brother is a bit of a wanker."

"By his brother, do you mean the King of England?" I asked, smiling despite the chaos of today's events.

"Naturally." Spencer brushed a kiss over my lips and my fingernails dug into his chest.

"It sounds like you don't like him much," I whispered, my thoughts already drifting from the royals and their problems.

"I don't," he confirmed, angling his mouth so I could nearly taste him. He pressed closer and I felt his hard cock nudging into my lower belly. My core tingled in anticipation of being alone with him. Our day-to-day was full of stolen moments like this, but I couldn't help but feel on edge as we stood in the middle of the Belmond drawing room. Anyone could walk in and ruin the moment. We were never truly alone anywhere we went in London. A maid had even accidentally walked in on us in our suite at the Westminster Royal a few weeks ago.

"Iris is home," I warned him. The warm spice of his cologne filled my nostrils. I wanted to bury my face into his chest and breathe him in. Spencer seemed to be having similar thoughts, because he bent and lifted me off my feet.

I suddenly didn't care if we were in the drawing room. There was only him. I circled my legs around his waist, nestling myself against the hard length of his shaft. Spencer's mouth captured mine, claiming it slowly. I opened to him, allowing his tongue to slide against mine. He sucked languidly for a moment until my hips began to rock with the pulse building inside me. I wanted him. I always wanted him. His mouth drew away but before I could complain his teeth caught my lower lip. He bit down gently and I moaned. Any lingering resistance melted away. I could only think of having him inside me.

"I need you," I whispered, my hands digging into his broad shoulders.

"You have me." There was a dangerous edge to his words that I guessed had something to do with Beatrice. Later, I'd ask him about their history. Now I just wanted him to prove what he claimed. That he belonged to me, even if it was only temporary.

I dipped a hand down, fumbling with his belt as he kissed me hungrily. I'd just unbuckled it when he placed me on my feet. Before I could protest, Spencer spun me around and bent me over the edge of the sofa Beatrice had sat on moments ago.

"I've been thinking about this all day," he rasped as he shoved my skirt around my hips.

I bit my lower lip, stifling a cry of pleasure at the sound

of his zipper being pulled down. A strong hand pinned my hip to the sofa arm and then I felt his tip breach my swollen sex. I pressed my mouth against my arm, afraid I wouldn't be able to control my volume as he drove into me. I swallowed a sob as I stretched around him. He filled me, his cock pushing its way so deeply inside of me that it almost hurt.

"Do you know how distracted I am at the office?" he continued, a finger stroking along the crack of my ass. He grabbed my cheeks and pushed them open wider as if he wanted to see himself inside me. "All I can think about is being buried inside you. I think about this—about stroking in and out of your warm, tight pussy—until you come. That's my favorite part. Do you know why?"

He thrust carefully, moving with slow deliberate motion as he spoke. I didn't trust myself to speak, so I shook my head, not daring to move my mouth from the arm that smothered my whimpers.

"Because I love watching you unravel. I love how your greedy pussy drains every drop out of me. It's all I can think about. I find myself thinking of new ways to undo you. New ways to fill you." He plunged his cock until I felt his balls smack against my sex. Spencer leaned down, his strong body covering mine as he whispered in my ear. "I want to fill every part of you, even this."

I felt his thumb press against the tight pucker of my ass. I tensed at the unexpected intrusion.

Spencer kissed my earlobe, pausing with his finger still in place. "I won't hurt you. Just tell me to stop."

"Don't," I gasped, willing my limbs to loosen under his body. "Don't stop."

"That's my girl." I heard the smile in his voice, which relaxed me even more. I'd pleased him and I would be rewarded. He massaged the spot, slowly increasing the pressure until he pushed inside me. I had to bite my arm to stop the unearthly pleasure clawing up my throat. Spencer kept his thumb there as he increased his pace. His cock slid into my heat and with each thrust, he coaxed his finger deeper. Pressure built with each stroke. My body tightened around him, waiting for the final release.But instead of bringing me to it with his cock, he paused with his erection rooted deep, and then he began to plunge his thumb instead.

I cracked open and spilled out. My body went limp save for the contractions of my pussy around him. I'd never experienced anything so intense in my life. Every atom of my being was centered on the point of my pleasure. After a moment, he began to move again, dragging his teeth across my shoulder as he grunted out his own climax. I felt it lash hot inside me. I never wanted it to end. I never wanted any of this to end. Maybe someday he wouldn't want me anymore, but I was his for as long as he would have me—in any way he wanted me.

So, when he whispered in my ear, "Come to the country with me."

I already knew my answer.

8

———

As I suspected, Hensley House was less of a house and more of a castle. It had taken nearly five hours for us to reach Yorkshire, mostly owing to a number of unplanned stops. Spencer wanted to show me some of his favorite spots, which had turned out to be an excuse to shag in every field we encountered. Not that I was complaining. By the time we pulled up the drive to Hensley, I was equal parts exhausted and content. Neither feeling lasted very long.

"What is he doing here?" Spencer's angry question roused me from my daze. I followed his attention to a car parked in front of the entrance to the estate.

"Is that...?" But I already recognized Holden's Land Rover. Apparently, we weren't the only ones who'd decided to flee the city. "Did you know he would be here?"

"No," Spencer said angrily, smacking his palm against the steering wheel, "but I shouldn't be surprised. I'm sure that Beatrice invited him."

"Then he can stay with her," I suggested.

Spencer tossed a harassed look in my direction before shaking his head. "That's an even worse idea. The two of them have history."

"Oh." I'd been tiptoeing around Spencer's relationship with Beatrice since her unexpected visit. Why did it feel worse knowing Holden was also involved?

"He royally fucked her over—like he does to every woman he dates."

"Really?" I couldn't help being a little surprised. Fucking someone over implied more than casual sex and flings. Everything Spencer had told me about his brother suggested a rather laissez-faire attitude where feelings were concerned, at least when it came to women.

"He's left a trail of devastation across the English landscape," Spencer said bitterly. "You know how he is."

Except, I didn't. I didn't know the Holden that Spencer knew. I'd seen glimpses of him, but in the short periods I'd spent in private with his brother, I'd discovered a man far more complicated than anyone seemed to realize. Maybe it wasn't so out of the ordinary to think he broke hearts as a hobby. He was clearly looking for love.

"It's fine," Spencer said, and I got the impression it was more for his benefit than mine. "There are twenty guest rooms. We can avoid him."

Twenty guest rooms. My eyes widened as I swept over Hensley House and took in the buildings and its lush grounds. The house itself boasted a Jacobethan style that made it appear all the more grandiose. Looking at it, it was impossible to decide if it was hundreds of years old or an example of the revival of the style. The exterior consisted of terra-cotta brickwork broken by arched windows. A few towers rose toward the sky, surrounded by parapets, breaking up the steeply gabled roofs. It was magnificent and intimating all at once, which I supposed was the point. But most of all, it was huge. Half a London city block would likely fit inside the interior. The grounds continued past the house replete with carefully-trimmed shrubbery that blocked a view of what lay beyond the hedges. It wasn't a country house. It was an estate, and further evidence that the Byrd family had deep roots in old English money. I continued to stare after Spencer helped me out of the car, momentarily distracted from the unwanted third member of the party. At least, until my gaze swept to my left and landed on Holden's SUV. Maybe Spencer was right and we could avoid Holden for the next two weeks, but I doubted it. Not because there wasn't enough space, but because Holden wasn't likely to allow that to happen. He wanted to stir up trouble as often as possible. In truth, Hensley was little more than a large cage that I was willingly stepping foot inside despite knowing that I would be trapped there with two men who brought out the primal instincts in each other.

What could go wrong?

MY QUESTION WAS ANSWERED within the hour. Spencer showed me inside Hensley with the characteristic oblivion I'd begun to expect from the wealthy people I found myself surrounded by. The interior of Hensley matched the exterior in terms of scale. Plush, Persian carpets the size of small flats were arranged artfully on the polished wood floors like a luxurious walkway. Paintings hung on the oak-paneled walls signed by artists whose names made me gasp. There had to be enough art to open a small museum in the foyer alone.

"That's the sitting room," Spencer said, pointing into a cavernous room. Three lonely sofas that looked both posh and uncomfortable were arranged around a grand fireplace with a marble hearth that took up a good portion of the southern wall. Tables and lamps dotted the space, some positioned around more chairs to offer ample seating. It looked like a room one might expect to find walking into a Jane Austen novel. Spencer didn't seem to notice my quiet awe as he continued, "The dining room. Although I prefer to take my meals on my veranda."

I nodded, swallowing as I took in the formal table and the twenty or more chairs placed around it. I could see why he preferred to eat somewhere less ostentatious. After that there was a study and a morning room, a library and a game room. I lost track of the dizzying number of spaces and found myself glad when he led me toward the stairs. From the second floor, a balcony looked out over the entry. We continued past it, turning once to head toward the east wing of the house. By the time we'd passed six bedrooms, I was beginning to wonder if I might actually get lost in this house. I didn't dare mention my fear to Spencer, because Kerrigan Belmond would have been to plenty of such estates in her life. I, however, felt like I'd wandered onto the set of a period drama.

"Holden's room is in the west wing," Spencer informed me when he finally paused in front of a door. "We should have our privacy."

Given the size of Hensley, he might as well have said that Holden's room was in Scotland. I had no doubt that I wouldn't hear so much as a peep from Holden unless we were on the main floor.

"The servants are in the basement," Spencer went on, and I blanched at the term. He noticed and quickly corrected himself, "I mean staff. Old habits."

Naturally, he'd been born to a family that still used terms like servants but it still left a sour taste in my mouth. Spencer was polite most of the time, but then again, I'd rarely seen him engage with any of the household staff at his grandfather's London home. I felt certain he employed a cleaning person to care for his flat in the city, but I had never encountered one. The truth was that there was a clear separation between him and those his family employed. I wondered that I'd never noticed it before.

"This is my room," he said, turning the knob and opening the door. "Or it is now."

The room wasn't quite what I expected it to be. A small desk with a Tiffany lamp sat near the window. A stack of newspapers had been left, presumably placed there prior to our arrival. The bed itself was much smaller than the one in Spencer's flat in London, although it held a plethora of comfortable looking pillows and was covered in plush linens. On one wall there was an antique wardrobe and on the other an unlit hearth. After taking in so much of Hensley, I was surprised at its elegant simplicity.

"We'll share a washroom," he said, opening a door next to the wardrobe, "but there are separate toilets and you have your own bathing chamber."

"My own..." I looked at him with confusion. "Aren't we sharing a room?"

"We could if you want, but mother thought we should take the master quarters," he explained. "Grandfather rarely comes up here, and she felt with our engagement..."

I swallowed as I realized that I'd already been promoted within Spencer's family. "I suppose I hadn't expected that to happen so quickly."

"Honestly, neither did I," he agreed. "It's a little insane that they still do things like this in old houses, isn't it? I forget that you grew up without the pleasures of the bloody aristocracy dictating propriety." He shot me a lop-sided grin that eased my mind a little. Kerrigan had been raised amongst a wealthy family, but this would be a little new to her.

Spencer took my hand and led me through the shared washroom into a second bedroom that was as opposite his room as night and day. His bedroom had been masculine, hewn down to the necessities with an eye for comfort, but my bedroom had been outfitted for a princess. In the center of the room, an oversized four-poster bed was piled with decorative pillows in a variety of golden yellow silks and brocades. Thick curtains were tied to each post and could be drawn for complete privacy. A velvet chaise with an artfully tossed blanket waited next to a marble hearth that held a large vase brimming with white roses, peonies, and other, smaller flowers. The walls were papered in a slightly textured pattern that shimmered with a golden sheen. Under one large window, sat a vanity stocked with expensive face creams, brushes, and a gilt mirror. Under the other window, was a polished writing desk inlaid with ivory.

"It's beautiful," I said truthfully, each moment catching sight of some small luxury that had been carefully considered for its mistress. "But am I supposed to sleep in that big bed alone?"

"I'd prefer you didn't." Spencer wrapped his arms around my waist and drew me to him. "I believe this particular arrangement speaks to years of arranged marriages."

I went rigid, realizing why his mother had insisted we use these rooms. It wasn't a gesture of acceptance. It was an acknowledgement that his relationship with Kerrigan was a contract between two powerful families. There was no expectation of love—not even a shared bed.

"What's wrong?" he asked.

"Sometimes I forget that we don't really have a say in our marriage," I admitted softly. "Everything was planned for us, even this room."

He was quiet for a moment, and I realized the significance of being given these quarters had been lost on him.

"I wasn't thinking," Spencer said, tightening his hold on me. "I should have told her we'd prefer a shared room."

"It's fine," I said quickly. The last thing I needed to do was stir up trouble. Kerrigan wouldn't. "As long as you sleep in my bed."

"That I can do." He kissed the top of my head. "And just think, you can kick me out if I snore."

"Or if I'm mad at you," I pointed out.

"Well, now I'm liking this private bedroom thing less and less." He spun me in his arms. "I think it's better to go to bed together if we're angry with each other."

"And why is that?" I asked, taking his obvious bait.

"Because then we can make up."

"Is that so?" I arched my eyebrow. "And how will a bed help with that?"

"Let me show you." Spencer lifted me up and carried me to the bed, dropping me into its cloud-like mattress before pouncing on top of me.

"But I'm hungry," I said with a pout, not bothering to show an ounce of resistance. The look in his eyes told me I would be rewarded for my patience.

He smirked. "So am I."

Spencer crawled down the length of my body, dropping kisses along his path. Even through the filmy fabric of my dress, I felt the heat of his mouth as he journeyed southward. He stopped when he reached my hips. Pushing onto an elbow, he lifted the hem of my skirt leaving me bare to the waist.

"I'm so glad I convinced you to ditch the knickers," he drawled, his eyes lingering on me.

I flushed under his gaze, feeling deliciously exposed. He slid a hand between my thighs and coaxed them apart. "Ah, my lunch has arrived," he said in a gruff voice that made my core clench. "I'm famished."

Spencer's head dropped down and my eyes closed at the first lash of his tongue along my swollen seam. After our numerous stops on our drive, I was sore, but my body still responded eagerly as he urged me open and continued to explore me with his lips and tongue. My legs fell open to him and Spencer moved his body to allow his mouth better access. Strong hands stretched me open and I moaned as his tongue thrust inside me.

My hands fisted into the silk coverlet and I held on as he consumed me. His mouth fucked me with relentless dedication as if to prove he'd meant it when he claimed to be hungry. The rough way he claimed me hurt a little given my soreness, but there was no resisting it. He drove me forward, past the slight discomfort to a place where all I could feel was him and the pleasure he gave me. My breaths turned to shallow pants, my muscles coiling, and as my body stretched to the breaking point, the wet heat of his mouth vanished. In an instant, Spencer was on top of me. He shoved a strong arm under my waist, lifting my hips, and rammed inside me.

I shattered around him, falling to pieces as my body and mind clung to where our bodies joined. Through the haze, I heard his breath catch and I threw my arms around his neck, holding on to his shoulders as he emptied inside me.

We stayed like that for a long moment, covered in sweat, before Spencer lowered his lips to mine. I'd begun to expect the unexpected in our lovemaking. When I was with him, he was completely in control. I literally came along for the ride. But it was the bittersweet moments after that I relished when he kissed me softly and whispered secrets to me.

"Are you still hungry?" he asked, smiling as he kissed down my jaw and moved to nibble my ear.

"Yes, but I'm not certain I can move," I admitted. My whole body felt as though it had turned into a puddle underneath him.

"We could take this off," he suggested, plucking the sleeve of the dress I still wore, even though it had been pushed to my waist. "You could stay naked in this bed and I could bring you something to eat."

"And then?"

"And then, nothing. We repeat the cycle as often as necessary. Maybe throw in some sleep and trips to the loo." He followed his offer with a kiss that left me seriously considering it.

"And what about your friends?" I said, reminding him of the reason that we were here in the first place.

"They can feed themselves." He nuzzled into my neck, making it harder to think of any more reasons that we shouldn't do exactly as he suggested.

But there was one more obligation that seemed likely to interfere with the plan. "And your brother?"

"I don't give a fuck what he does," Spencer growled, but before I could diffuse the bomb I'd accidentally triggered a loud guffaw startled us apart.

"I am wounded."

I scrambled, trying to push my dress back over my naked lower half. Spencer assisted but barely moved from the spot where he lay beside me. Pushing up on my elbows, I discovered Holden standing in the open doorway to the shared washroom. There was no use asking how long he'd been there. The devious smirk on his face answered for me.

"Get out," Spencer said in a low voice that sounded

surprisingly bored at his brother's presence. "And learn to knock."

"Learn to close a door if you're going to fuck like bunnies." Holden ignored his brother and stepped inside the room. "I just came by to say hello and offer you some lunch, but then I found you already eating."

"And you didn't think to give us some privacy?" Spencer finally bothered to sit up, shoving his half-spent cock back into his pants but not bothering to refasten his trousers.

"It would be rude to just leave." Holden lounged against the armoire, his thumbs hooking on the pockets of his jeans. "Besides I thought you might want me to join you."

"Join?" I spluttered, my hand instinctively pushing my dress between my already clamped thighs.

"That won't be necessary," Spencer said, his weariness taking a dangerous edge. "And I'll thank you to stay out of our bedrooms."

"I see," Holden said coolly, but his eyes skipped over to me. "And what about you, dirty girl? Do you want me to stay out of your room?"

"Yes," I snapped.

"Alright." He shrugged, his broad shoulders straining against the cotton of his black t-shirt. "But you're always welcome in my room. Consider it an open invitation."

"She sends her regrets," Spencer bit back.

"Now, now." Holden's eyes stayed fixed on mine. "That's for her to decide. Right, dirty girl?"

"Get out," I echoed Spencer's earlier command, my

fingers straying toward a pillow. Was it immature to throw it at him? Probably. But since he seemed incapable of taking hints or following direct orders, I lobbed it at him anyway.

Holden ducked out of the way with a laugh, opening his mouth with what was sure to be another clever retort. The mistake cost him as my next pillow hit him square in the face. This time, he held up his hands in surrender and backed out of the room, leaving me and Spencer alone. For now.

9

"He doesn't mean anything by it," Spencer said as he tucked in his shirt.

"What?" I asked, spinning from the wardrobe with a pair of jeans in my hands. I'd opted to change out of the dress I'd worn in the car. After being on display in front of Holden, I found myself wanting both a fresh pair of knickers as well as a thick layer of denim covering me up. The more barriers between us, the better.

Spencer had been quiet since Holden had left the room. I'd assumed he was simply seething with barely contained rage, but there wasn't even a hint of anger in his voice now. "He's just testing his boundaries."

"Toddlers test their boundaries!" I couldn't believe I was hearing this from him. Spencer had made it clear that he wanted me to stay away from his brother. He'd even kicked him out of the flat the two shared, which probably accounted for how he'd wound up here. Now he was defending him? I didn't know what to make of either of the

Byrd brothers. Just when I thought I had one of them figured out, the rug was pulled out from under me. "He watched us have sex."

Spencer shrugged, tugging loose a cufflink. He deposited it on the bedside table and rolled up the sleeve. Apparently, this was as casual as he was going to get. "It's nothing he hasn't seen before."

"It'... nothing..." I couldn't believe what I was hearing. "Do you mean the sex or my vagina? Because he's never seen me naked or us having sex before."

"He's seen me having sex before, and well, he's seen some of you."

"Do you even hear how fucked up that sounds?" I yanked up my jeans and reached for a light sweater. Autumn had arrived in Yorkshire ahead of us, and I already found myself wishing I'd brought warmer clothing for the cooler temperatures.

"I'm sure from the outside—"

"From any side," I cut him off. I forced myself to pause and take a deep breath. I had complicated feelings where the two of them were concerned, especially when it came to sexual attraction. But I'd been doing my best to consider Spencer's feelings. Suddenly, I didn't know what that meant anymore. "Look, you told me that you didn't want to share me and now, you're acting like..."

"I don't want to share you," Spencer admitted. "But I can't blame him for wanting you. I want you all the time."

"Actually, you can," I stared at him. "He's your brother. He shouldn't be trying to steal your fiancée."

Spencer's head tilted to the side, an amused expression playing on his face. "He's not trying to steal you. He's trying to sleep with you. He knows you belong to me."

My mouth went dry. For the first time, in weeks I wished the year was nearly up. I wasn't sure how much longer I could survive this wild ride.

"What's wrong?" Spencer asked after a few moments of silence.

"Nothing," I lied. "I just expected you to be more upset."

Spencer took my hands, knitting them together. "Look, I've learned to choose my battles. You and I have made a commitment to each other that's going to last a lot longer than this infatuation Holden has with you."

"Will it?" I asked absently.

His jaw set in a hard line and he nodded. "At least, I hope so." He paused, softening a little. "I don't want there to be any regrets for either of us. I should have handled things better."

"Spencer," I said carefully, "you realize that it's not right. The sharing, I mean."

"Who gets to define what's right?" he asked curiously. "You? Me? The world?"

"I just don't think..." But I didn't know what to think or not think. Not anymore. I'd been sucked into temptation with them both once before. I'd thought we'd drawn a clear line in the sand, but the thing about sand was that it was just as easy to erase a line as it was to create it.

"We're going to be married, which is a first for both of us. But it's a first for both of us—as brothers, I mean," he clarified. "I have different responsibilities now and I need to think about my career. It needed to end."

Sadness formed a lump in my throat. "Is that all this is: a career decision?"

"No." He squeezed my hands. "I want you all to myself, too. But sometimes…"

"What?" I blinked against the tears threatening to spill down my cheeks.

Spencer took a step closer, bending his head so that his lips brushed against my ear. "I love to give you pleasure. I love to watch you come undone. You know that, right?"

"Yes," I whispered.

"I can never give you the pleasure that *we* can give you." His lips grazed my jaw, and my eyes shuttered, drinking in his words and his touch. "Four hands on your body touching you, leaving nothing unexplored. Two mouths kissing you, tasting every inch of your skin." He paused to let his words sink in and I moaned. "And two cocks filling you until you think you can't take any more and you lose all control. I can't give you that alone."

My teeth sank into my lower lip, my breathing growing shallow as I imagined the picture he painted. It wasn't the first time I'd fantasized about being with both of them, but hearing it from his point of view shifted my perspective. I'd felt selfish for wanting it before, assuming it was all about me. Now I realized that was exactly why Spencer liked it.

But there was one thing I couldn't understand. "Why him? Why your brother?"

Spencer drew back, and I opened my eyes to find his cold emerald gaze pinned on me. "Because, despite our differences, he's the only person I can trust. I've worked hard to carry the family legacy. I've given up most of the vices Spencer enjoys. I won't throw away everything I've worked for, so discretion is key."

"Oh." I didn't hide my surprise at his answer. In a way, it made sense. It wasn't until we reached the first floor that I processed what he said. *He's the only person I can trust.*

I couldn't help but wonder if that was before he met me.

10

We found Holden on the veranda, absorbed in something on his phone and ignoring the breathtaking vista surrounding us. A large hedge maze stretched to the perimeter of the grounds where it met hills speckled with groves of trees. Their leaves had begun to change, shedding their youthful green for rich shades of garnet, bronze, and marigold. I wondered if I could find my way through the labyrinth out to the beautiful wild beyond it. But I found myself more drawn to the table, where Holden sat. Not because of his presence, but rather the luncheon spread across it. Platters, trays, and bowls that looked suspiciously like real silver were heaped with fresh fruit, puddings, and other delicacies that made my stomach growl so loudly that I blushed. Holden looked up from his phone. Despite the aviators he wore, there was no hiding the surprise written across his face.

"Was that your stomach?" Before I could answer, he

turned to his brother. "You should take better care of your fiancée, she sounds like she's starving to death."

"That's why I brought her down for lunch." Spencer pulled out a chair for me, not sparing so much as a glance at his brother.

"You're welcome for having this put out," Holden said caustically.

"Thank you." Spencer took a seat next to mine. "Although, you might have mentioned you were going to be at Hensley."

"I didn't know that I needed your permission to come to our family estate." Holden slid a tray of sandwiches toward me, sparing a quick look at me. "Eat something before you pass out. I would have had lunch waiting if I knew you were coming."

I didn't wait for them to finish their argument before I started heaping things on my plate. I snatched a few cucumber sandwiches from the silver platter then moved on to a bowl of cut fruit. They were still bickering when I took my first bite, but it tasted too good for me to care. I continued eating until I realized both men had stopped talking and turned their attention to me.

I swallowed the melon in my mouth. "What?"

"You were hungry," Holden said, the corner of his mouth dancing.

"She worked up an appetite," Spencer lounged back in his seat, popping a grape into his mouth.

My eyes narrowed at the suggestive turn this was taking, but I didn't waste time participating in their double entendre. Instead, I swiped another sandwich from the platter and let them continue their endless squabbling. In a way, after what Spencer had revealed, their rivalry was almost cute. I'd begun to see that I'd gotten the wrong impression about them. Spencer needed to consider his career and start getting serious. Holden wanted to keep having fun. I couldn't exactly blame either of them, but I wished they would stop fighting with each other and have a serious conversation. There had to be a middle ground for both of them. I nibbled at the sandwich, wondering what that might be.

"I should have ordered more," Holden noted when I polished off the final sandwich from the tray.

"I refuse to apologize for eating," I told him.

"I wouldn't want you to," he said with an amused grin. "But I'll make sure to have the kitchen make more sandwiches tomorrow."

I sincerely doubted that I would be as hungry tomorrow as I was right now. There had to be less shagging in fields now that we were in Yorkshire, but it hardly seemed polite to point that out.

"I can speak to the kitchens. Don't bother yourself," Spencer said coolly. There was nothing cute in the gaze he leveled at Holden. He was drawing a line in the sand between them and placing me firmly behind it.

Holden placed his mobile on the table, his own plate still untouched, and smiled, completely unfazed. "Drink?"

"Whiskey," Spencer said.

Holden turned to me, but I shook my head. It was way too early in the day for me to risk drinking, especially with both of them there. He disappeared into the main house, leaving Spencer and me alone. I sagged in relief as some of the tension in the air dissipated.

"I thought we could drive up to the village when you're finished, but first you should try this." Spencer deposited a decadent chocolate cake onto my plate. "I dreamt about this pudding while I was at university. It's a local specialty."

"Didn't make it to Yorkshire much back then?"

"Too busy. I took two advanced degrees. There wasn't time for the country," he explained. Although he tried to hide it, I detected a note of bitterness.

I cut into the cake with my fork and took a bite. Instantly, I moaned. The sponge of the cake hid a creamy layer of chocolate custard that was so decadent I felt I might need forgiveness for the sounds I was making.

"Told you," Spencer said with a genuine smile as I finished off the cake. He was still grinning when I took the last bite.

There was something so utterly disarming about the way he watched me that I found myself leaning across the table to kiss him before I'd swallowed the last bit.

Our mouths lingered in the kiss for a moment, before he straightened in his chair. "Holden used to send me photos of it when he came here for holidays."

I gasped in mock outrage. "And he didn't bring you any?"

"Never. The bastard," Spencer said with a laugh.

I loved these small glimpses into their lives. The ones that showed me that they loved each other as much as they pissed each other off. It helped me worry less about the digs and insults they hurled at each other the rest of the time.

Still, I couldn't quite shake the feeling that their rivalry was coming to a head. I didn't know what direction that would send their relationship. Seeing him smile gave me hope that they would come out stronger on the other side.

"What?" Spencer asked, angling his head to study me. "What's that smile for?"

"I was just thinking that it's nice that you have a brother—whether or not you think so," I added with a roll of my eyes. "The story about the cake. It just reminded me of the night we watched football together."

Spencer's mouth tightened. "That was a memorable night."

"Oh!" My hand flew to my mouth. "Not because of that." I flushed as I tried to ignore the memories his reaction had dredged to mind.

"It's okay. I don't exactly regret that night," Spencer said in an even tone. "But it does remind me that I had something I'd been meaning to ask you."

My mouth went dry as I considered all the possible questions that night might remind him to ask. I reached for my water glass, nodding for him to continue.

"Why does he call you dirty girl?" Spencer asked in a lowered voice.

My stomach plummeted so hard, I thought it might actually hit the ground. I'd hoped that Spencer hadn't caught that little nickname earlier, even though Holden had clearly meant for him to hear it.

But before I could answer, Holden did it for me. He prowled to the table and handed Spencer one of the drinks he carried. "I guess it just stuck from that lunch date."

"Lunch date?" Spencer stared at me. Betrayal darkened his eyes for a moment and then vanished like clouds passing over the sun on a summer's day.

"The date wasn't with him," I said, quickly taking a sip of water and wishing I'd taken Holden up on a stronger drink. "I was with Iris and your mother. Evie was there."

"And so was Holden?" This time the thick confusion sounded less wounded.

"It was a coincidence." I shrugged my shoulders, hoping we would leave soon for the village—before Holden could plant more suggestions in his brother's head.

"I think fate simply took a hand," Holden drawled. He swished his whiskey and the brown liquid nearly spilled over the cut-crystal glass. Almost. I was starting to understand that Holden was more in control than he let on. I suspected he always was, actually. "Put you and me in that loo at the same time."

"What?" Spencer asked, looking between the two of us.

I couldn't speak. I couldn't think of a thing to say. This wasn't happening.

"It's a great story." Holden winked at me over his brother's shoulder. "Do you want to tell it or should I?"

"It's not a story. It's a figment of your imagination," I snapped at him, finally finding my voice. I couldn't imagine how Holden's delusions might color the events of that day. The truth was that he had no idea what I'd done in that bathroom stall. He hadn't seen me touching myself. "Besides, I already told Spencer about it."

"You did?" Holden actually looked surprised.

"I did," I bluffed, there was no point in telling him that

I'd left a few things out. "I thought it was him that day, who sent me the note and champagne. He cleared it up for me."

"Is that all you told him?" Holden pressed.

"Now I am interested," Spencer said and his shoulders relaxed a little. Maybe he did trust me a bit. "Why did you send her a note?"

I wasn't sure how long that trust would last.

"Well, I was at an insufferably long luncheon with those investors from Quinn's group."

Spencer nodded as if all of this information made sense to him and I braced myself for what came next.

"Rose was working the bar," he continued, and I stiffened at the mention of the pretty blonde. Rose hadn't just been some waitress from Hillgrove's. I'd officially met her at the flat the brothers shared the day after I'd given Spencer my virginity. That morning, she'd informed me that Holden wasn't the only Byrd she'd slept with. "Anyway, I lured her off to the loo."

"And what does this have to do with Kerrigan?" Spencer flicked a fly off his plate, already looking bored.

"Rose and I thought we were alone, so naturally we took advantage of the situation." He winked at me again. "Didn't we, dirty girl?"

"Stop calling me that."

Holden pretended to frown. "I thought you liked it. I mean, you certainly earned the nickname."

"How?" Spencer sat up, looking a bit more interested. "Did she join you two?"

"What? No!" I crossed my arms over my chest. "Holden is telling the story wrong. I was in the loo, minding my own business, when the two of them came in and started shagging. I had nothing to do with it."

"But you stayed," Holden pointed out. Our eyes met and no matter how hard I tried, I couldn't look away from him.

"I was trapped," I spat back. "What was I supposed to do?"

"Leave." Both the men answered at once.

"I didn't want to interrupt," I mumbled.

Spencer's eyebrows furrowed and I braced myself, but instead of getting angry, he only laughed. "How polite of you."

"Anyway, she was in there listening the whole time, staying quiet as a church mouse." Holden took a swig of his drink.

"And what does this have to do with her nickname?"

Holden's mouth curved into a crooked grin. "I thought I heard someone when I was leaving, but she didn't answer when I called out. I was about to leave when I heard her mobile go off. I had no idea who she was so I told her that she could have joined us, called her a dirty girl, and left. Imagine my surprise when a few minutes later, I spot your arranged fiancée ducking out of the loo with a face the color of a fire engine. So I sent some champagne to the table to cool her down."

Spencer looked between the two of us. "That's the whole story?"

"That's my side of the story." Holden leaned forward in his seat, planting his elbows on the table. "But I'd love to hear what you were doing in there. Or maybe you could show us, dirty girl."

"No thanks, I don't feel like vomiting at the moment," I said coldly.

"I think I would have heard that." But he sat back in his seat looking defeated.

Spencer grabbed another grape and popped it into his mouth thoughtfully. "I'm sorry, Kerrigan. That must have been a harrowing thirty, maybe forty seconds you had to experience."

I choked on the drink I'd just taken, nearly spraying water over the table with laughter at the unexpected dig.

"That hurts." Holden pressed a hand to his chest. "It was at least ninety seconds, brother."

I looked from one to the other, feeling for the first time, that maybe we could all get along. Then I delivered one final, good-natured blow. "Sixty seconds at best."

11

"We'll stay for dinner and then we'll leave," Spencer promised me as we wound through the country roads leading us to Welbatten Hall. Twilight crept across the landscape, painting the world in muted, golden hues as the sun fled the sky.

"If you want." I fiddled with the button hole on my jacket, the evening had begun to cool, another sign that summer was all but a fleeting memory. "We can stay as long as you like."

Spencer glanced at me, his hands firmly gripping the steering wheel, and grimaced. "If it was up to me, we wouldn't go at all. I would be taking my supper in bed."

"That sounds messy." I stopped playing with my button and moved my hand to his knee. "Do you normally do that in the country?"

"Never." He grinned and my heart did a little flip. "But you're what I want for supper."

"Oh." I bit my lower lip, feeling an increasingly familiar

surge of arousal at the suggestive tone in his voice. "In that case, I wish we'd stayed in, too." I turned my attention out the window, watching the country fly by and sighed as my fingers began to dance impatiently.

"What's wrong?" he asked.

"Why do you think something's wrong?"

"Because you're drumming my knee," he said.

"Sorry!" I stopped my fidgeting and did my best to keep my hand still, sliding my palm up his thigh where it could rest flatly.

"Well, now you're giving me ideas." He lowered a hand to cover mine as if to lock it in place. "But, honestly, you seem preoccupied, Kerrigan."

I couldn't help but think of what I would find if I slid my hand just a little farther up, but the idea wasn't enough to distract me from my nerves. Each minute in the car seemed to make me more and more anxious. With Spencer next to me I had an anchor that kept me from being pulled under into a full-blown panic attack.

"Are you sure I'm dressed properly?" I blurted out. It was actually something worrying me, if not the primary cause for my concern.

"You look beautiful," he reassured me.

That wasn't what I asked but I preened a little under the compliment. After grilling Spencer on what to expect this evening, and Holden interjected his own thoughts, I'd opted for a cream silk blouse paired with trim, tailored black trousers that stopped just above my ankle and black Louboutin stilettos. Over it, I'd opted for a camel-colored cashmere jacket that felt like butter on my skin. I'd dared to leave a few buttons unfastened on my shirt to give glimpses of both my décolletage and the armor I wore under the sophisticated ensemble. My black lace bra cupped my breasts into delicate submission. In the right light, its outline could be seen through the lighter fabric of my shirt, which was exactly how I planned it. Spencer wouldn't be able to keep his eyes off me, which is what I really wanted, particularly with Beatrice around.

But, given that a Prince was going to be at tonight's fête, I wondered if I looked too informal. I hadn't been worried until Spencer had opted for a dinner jacket.

None of that was what really weighed on me, though. This was the first time I had to navigate a social encounter with someone who knew Kerrigan well, and I was doing so without Giles nearby. Although, I had my mobile tucked securely in my clutch in case of emergency. I hoped I was right and that any slip-ups would be excused by Kerrigan's lengthy separation from Beatrice.

"He's just another man," Spencer said, calling me from my thoughts.

"Who? Holden?" I asked in confusion.

"Edward," he said, his eyes darting to me and then back to the ever-darkening road. "That's why you're so anxious, right?"

I exhaled and seized the excuse readily. "Yes. That's why. I've never met royalty before."

"I thought you and Bea used to hang with Priscilla at Woldingham."

It took me a second to realize he was referencing Priscilla Windsor, the daughter of one of King Albert's brothers. Of course, Kerrigan had gone to school with someone like her. Woldingham catered to England's elite. I wondered who else I was supposed to *know*.

"Oh, her. I meant real royals," I said without thinking.

But Spencer burst into laughter. "Oh god, I wish she could hear you say that. I've only met her a couple of times but she struck me as a real twat." He paused, regret instantly coloring his face. "I'm sorry. She was your friend. I shouldn't—"

"It's okay. I know a lot of twats," I told him. At least, I imagined Kerrigan did based on what I knew about her.

"It is nice to finally meet some of your friends, though," he tacked on thoughtfully.

"Yes, it is," I said absently, then remembered myself. "I've been so caught up in other things I haven't seen many of them since I returned."

Spencer lifted my hand to his lips and kissed it. "You mean us. I've been selfish keeping you all to myself."

"Who says it's not the other way around?" I asked.

"You want me all to yourself?" He spun the wheel, turning us down a dark, private lane.

I swallowed as the first lights came into view in the distance. Welbatten Hall. "Take me back to Hensley and I'll show you."

"Don't tempt me." He thought I was joking, but he was only half right.

It couldn't be coincidence that none of Kerrigan's friends had come to call until now. I'd met a few at parties and events, where there was plenty of safety in numbers. I suspected that Tod Belmond had arranged to keep me away from them the rest of the time. It was a move that I appreciated, but avoiding Kerrigan's old life couldn't continue forever, especially not for an entire year. As it was, I was getting daily prompts from Giles to post photos on Kerrigan's social media accounts to keep up appearances. And then there was the wedding date. I hadn't gotten the opportunity to speak with Tod before we left for Yorkshire. Maybe I'd even avoided him. Did I really want to know if Kerrigan would be back sooner than expected? What if she came back next month or next week? Tomorrow?

Was I ready to walk away from this life so suddenly?

"We're here," Spencer announced as we pulled in front of a Georgian manor. It was impossible to make out much of its architecture, its brick facade blending in too well with the night. Mostly it just struck me as large, but I couldn't help noting, with some satisfaction, not nearly as massive as Hensley House.

Spencer appeared at my side of the McLaren and helped me out, which was thoughtful given that my shoes didn't mix well with the pea-gravel drive. I noticed a few other cars parked alongside ours. I pointed to a Land Rover.

"It looks like Holden beat us."

"He's probably trying to get into Beatrice's knickers already," Spencer said with a shake of his head.

"I thought they hated each other."

Spencer snorted a laugh. "When has that ever stopped someone? Hate fucking is his particular brand of catnip."

"I see." Something about that made my stomach twist into knots given how often Holden came on to me. Did he hate me? Is that why he wanted to get me into bed?

And why should it bother me if so?

I pushed away the questions he'd raised, determined to focus on getting through the evening. When we reached the front door, a man wearing a black suit answered. I was about to greet him when he nodded and stepped to the side. I followed Spencer into the grand entry. The floor was tiled in black and white marble until it reached a sweeping staircase, leading to the upper floors. Nearby a polished mahogany table held a towering arrangement of tuberoses and lilies in a Chinese porcelain vase.

"Mr. Byrd and Miss Belmond, welcome. The other guests are in the lounge." He waited by the door expectantly. Spencer turned and shrugged off his overcoat into the man's waiting hands, which I noticed for the first time were gloved. Then Spencer turned and helped me with my jacket and passed it to the man, which I now presumed was the Highclere family's butler.

He moved away with the jackets over his arm, then paused, and looked at me. "And, if I may be so bold, it is lovely to have you back at Welbatten, Miss Belmond."

Oh, fuck me. Apparently, the fact that I'd been here before had either slipped Giles' mind or been unknown to him. I gathered myself and smiled brightly. "I'm glad to be back."

The butler paused, blinking his eyes for a moment, as if confused by something, and I readied myself to be called out on some small mistake. Instead, he tilted his head. "If you'll follow me."

Relief flooded through me as Spencer offered me his arm. I looped mine through his as we were shown to the lounge. It vanished as soon as we entered the room. Holden lounged on a brocade settee that looked like it had been around since the house was built. He looked at me over the rim of a whiskey glass and winked. Across from him Beatrice was chattering away at an overwhelmed man who I recognized from tabloid covers. For an instant, I felt like Kate, standing there and gawking like I might have if royalty had walked into the Hare & Hound. Then I remembered that Kerrigan Belmond used to hang out with princesses at boarding school and likely wouldn't be impressed by his presence, even if he was fourth in line to the throne.

"You're here!" Beatrice stood and rushed towards us. Out of the corner of my eye, I saw Edward's shoulders slump in relief.

Beatrice had clearly decided tonight was a festive affair, because she'd opted for a gold sequin jumpsuit that dipped between her breasts. Her blonde hair was piled into a topknot as flawless as her red lipstick and winged eyeliner. Something told me that she was an interested in a hate fuck as Holden. She couldn't be angling for Edward's attention, since he was both a recent widow and gay. Then again, considering how she was chatting him up and how relieved he looked that she'd been distracted, I could be wrong.

Was this what socializing amongst the fabulously wealthy and famous was like? Everyone counting the minutes until they could leave? It definitely didn't feel like the times I'd spent drinking wine late into the night with Eliza and her friends.

"Can I get you a drink?" she asked and I nodded gratefully.

"Wine," I said, not caring what she served me so long as it had alcohol.

"Seriously?" She flashed me the whites of her eyes. "This is a celebration. It calls for champagne." Before I could respond, she snapped her fingers over my shoulder.

I clamped my mouth closed so it wouldn't fall open at the condescending gesture. A moment later, a server approached me with a tray of champagne flutes. I took one, considering if I should grab a second now and down the first one like a shot. But he turned to deliver them to the others. Spencer took one, as did Edward, although the latter looked slightly queasy holding it.

Beatrice held her champagne over her head, the sequins of her outfit sending dazzling sparkles dancing around the room. "To old friends and new adventures."

I forced a grin and downed my champagne, my eyes skittering to find Edward wearing a tight-lipped smile of his own. I didn't know him, but everyone in England—in the world really—knew all the details of his personal life. Beatrice might have money and looks, but she certainly lacked the empathy to realize that the last thing her friend, if he was that at all, was a celebratory reunion with champagne and sequins.

The butler came in and Beatrice groaned. "Excuse me a moment. It seems I'm needed."

She sauntered over to speak with him. I saw my chance and unlooped my arm from Spencer's, whispering, "Give me a sec."

My heart pounded as I crossed the few steps to where Beatrice had sat a few minutes earlier. I paused, offering the warmest smile I could muster, and held out a hand. "We haven't been introduced yet. I'm Kerrigan. I knew Beatrice at Woldingham."

Edward took my hand and shook it gently, then gestured to the empty seat next to him. "Please sit down. In fact, I'm begging you to sit down before she gets back. I think Beatrice missed the memo that I'm not on the market...or rather, that I've never been on her market."

"I can sympathize. I think she forgets that Spencer is spoken for, too." I chuckled.

"Oh, that's right. I heard Spencer was engaged. You weren't at St. Andrews with us, though, were you?" he asked conversationally.

"No, I was at Oxford." It was easier and easier to slip into Kerrigan's history. Perhaps, because so little had happened to me in my life, I could adopt her past more readily. There was nothing to get mixed up over. But I knew I had to be careful. I might know the facts but there were plenty of details only she could know and remember.

"And you're settling for a St. Andrew's man?" he asked with the first genuine smile I'd seen from him. It changed his entire face, making him look years younger than he had when I'd first sat down. The Prince was good-looking and had a reputation as the more charming of England's royal men. Like his brother, he'd gotten his looks from his mother. A royal in her own right, the late Queen had been exiled from Greece before marrying their father. Both of Edward's parents had died tragically. It was another reason that I felt drawn to him, I suppose. We both understood loss, but I couldn't begin to imagine what he had gone through.

"You're a St. Andrew's man," Spencer pointed out, joining us. He stood next to me, placing a hand on my shoulder. I reached up instinctively and held it. Edward's eyes followed and lingered on our clasped hands.

He finally peeled his eyes away and grinned. It was all charm with no weight behind it. He'd slipped into the role he'd played most of his life. "I apologize for that fact often."

"We're not so bad," Spencer teased. He tipped his head back in the direction where Holden held residence with his whiskey. "Present company notwithstanding."

"Am I being insulted?" Holden called across the room.

"We're talking about St. Andrews," Spencer replied, not bothering to look at his brother. "That place we paid a King's ransom to give you a degree."

"I studied constantly at university, you know that?"

This time it was Edward who laughed, but his tone was good natured. "What did you study? I don't think you ever stepped foot in a library."

Holden sat up, leaning his elbows on his knees, and shrugged. His eyes met mine and locked on them. "The best lessons in life aren't taught in books or classrooms. They're lived."

"How profound," Spencer muttered. "What lessons did you learn?"

"Anatomy. Chemistry. Biology." He flashed his perfect teeth in a wide smile. "Women's Studies."

"I don't think that's what you think it is," I said dryly.

"I'd be happy to share what I learned on that subject." He took a long swig of whiskey, then got to his feet. "Anytime, *Kerrigan*."

Her name oozed off his tongue, each syllable drawn out and intentional. It was the first time he'd used it in weeks, since the accusation he'd made that night at Sparrow Court. Part of me had begun to relax, thinking I'd convinced him he was mental. But now I realized, he'd been biding his time while he waited for his moment. Holden Byrd was walking around with a bomb, and I had no idea when he might drop it.

Edward's eyes slid to me and back to Holden, then up to Spencer, but he didn't say anything. Was it that obvious that there were issues between the three of us? All the generosity I'd felt toward Holden this afternoon was quickly being depleted. It was one thing to act like a jackass, it was another thing to make it the primary purpose of your life.

"Dinner is ready!" Beatrice exclaimed, returning to the room completely oblivious to the tension around her.

She ushered us into the dining room where a table for twenty had been set for the five of us. Edward and Beatrice sat at opposite ends of the table. I was placed next to Spencer, or as close as the massive table allowed with Edward on my left, and Holden was across from us. It didn't escape my attention that Beatrice had a Byrd brother on either side of her. It seemed she wasn't all that interested in catching up with me or Edward, after all. That was fine by me as I had no real interest in her, but it was alarming how she seemed to flirt with both men in front of me, even knowing one was my fiancé.

At least, as far as she knew.

"So what have you been up to?" Beatrice directed her first round of questions at Spencer. "I never see you out. You can't work all the time."

"My position in my grandfather's office keeps me busy," he replied in a clipped tone.

"Ah, yes, Spencer Byrd, the future youngest Prime Minister," she said with a giggle, completely ignoring the soup that had just been placed before her.

I thanked the server for mine, but picking up my spoon I found my stomach churning too roughly to eat. I was out of my element. The ridiculous thing was that I'd been out of my element for weeks now, but I'd managed to find my footing with Spencer. At least, that's how it felt. I swirled my spoon in the bisque as I listened to Beatrice chatter away.

"You can't be seriously worried about that with a wedding to plan. Is he helping you with that, Kerrigan?"

I looked up, surprised to be brought into the conversation. She seemed fine keeping Spencer's attention all to herself. "Oh, um, our mothers are planning most of it."

"You mean Iris," Beatrice said her name with disdain. "I can't believe you'd let her. This is going to be the social event of the season. The biggest wedding since Alexander married Clara."

"Hopefully, less exciting," Edward muttered next to me, low enough that she couldn't hear.

I shot him a sympathetic look. Turning, I dropped my

voice. "I should tell you that I was really sorry to hear about your husband."

Edward stilled, save for the slide of his throat. Then, he nodded. "Thank you. It's been a rough year."

"What are you two whispering about?" Beatrice called.

"Nothing," I said quickly, not wanting her to add any more tactless remarks on the subject.

"No secrets amongst friends." She pretended to pout. "Tell them, Holden."

His mouth curved into a wry smile and he reached for his wine glass. "I'm staying out of this."

"Really, Edward, I want to hear everything," she continued. "There's so much catching up to do with all of us since we graduated. How have you been?"

I felt the urge to reach out and grab his hand to steady him through the encounter, but owing to the ridiculous formality of our dining arrangement that was impossible.

But Edward gave her a serene smile as he lifted his napkin to dab the corners of his mouth. He replaced it on his lap and answered, "Well, my husband is dead. So I've kinda been shit."

His words hit Beatrice like a gust of wind. She seemed to rise a little before collapsing into a mass of apologies. "I'm sorry, that was thoughtless of me. I just...thought we could all catch up, but, of course, I should have been more sensitive. Please—"

"Beatrice." Edward cut her off with a raised hand. "Let's just drop it. I don't want to talk about it."

"Of course." She nodded in agreement, waving a server over to take her barely touched soup. I was grateful when mine was lifted from the place in front of me, as well. "So, how is your brother then? And your new nephew?"

"They're fabulous," he said, snagging his wine glass and holding it up for a refill. "Might I get another glass?"

Somehow, I doubted he meant that. I also doubted that Beatrice was going to pick up on the fact that Edward didn't want to catch up or talk about his life. She must be blind not to see it, but perhaps that's just what happens when the world revolves around you long enough.

"Beatrice, what are you up to these days?" I jumped in, knowing that every narcissist's favorite topic was themself.

"Well, I've been working with the London historical trust," she began, and continued on through the main course and well after. It was both a reprieve and a punishment. Beatrice clearly found her days more fascinated than anyone who did absolutely fucking nothing, should. Holden used the time to drink a bottle of wine. Edward the same. I kept her talking, not bothering to eat much myself. That was until pudding arrived.

"Your eyes just lit up," Spencer murmured when the Yorkshire pudding he'd shared with me earlier was placed before me.

I sank my spoon into it and took a bite, sagging with pleasure. It felt like a reward after handling Beatrice through the whole soup course and following salmon entree. When I finally looked up, I found Holden watching me. His gaze lingered on my mouth, his eyes narrowed, and he shifted in his chair, finishing another glass of wine. There was something possessive in the way he surveyed me. Finally, his eyes lifted to meet mine and I found myself unable to turn away, just as I had the day at the bridal salon. Spencer had taken over with Beatrice and was too absorbed in feigning interest in the details of her upcoming philanthropy drive to notice Holden's naked interest.

Edward coughed, severing the connection, and I turned my face to my plate, shame burning on my cheeks.

"When are you getting married?" he asked me gently as though he was approaching an escaped horse that needed to be led back to its own pasture.

I lifted my brows, surprised that he would bring up weddings given what he had been through. "We'd talked about summer, but it seems our families want a holiday wedding."

"Holiday weddings are beautiful," he said in a thick voice. There was a flash of pain in his blue eyes and I saw him struggle to keep it under control. "There's really no point in waiting if you know it's right. Take the time that you have and hold on tightly. Love can be taken in an instant."

"I will," I promised him so softly that he probably couldn't even hear me, but he bobbed his head in approval. Part of me wished I could crack open and spill out all my secrets to him. There was something about the man that felt so comforting, like he could be my best friend, but this wasn't the time or place for that. And it would be a terrible position to put him in since he'd known Spencer for years.

As soon as we were finished, Beatrice announced cocktails would be served in the conservatory. I found myself longing for my small flat in West Bexby where dinner, drinks, and life were all carried out on one sofa in a tiny room. Maybe it was the arrangement I'd agreed to, but this world felt like wandering into a stage play. Every new scene needed to be played on a new set. There were even costume changes. Maybe that's why it had been so easy to slip into Kerrigan's life. She was playing a part, just like the rest of them. I was simply her understudy.

"I'm afraid I need to be going. My driver is waiting for me," Edward said apologetically when we reached the hall.

"But we'll see more of you. Promise!" Beatrice demanded shrilly, throwing her arms around his neck and nearly knocking him off balance.

I'd been stuck listening to her drone on about her life throughout dinner. She'd been so busy talking that she had barely eaten. She had gotten in a fair bit of drinking, however.

"Of course," he said quickly, prying himself free. He shook Spencer's hand and Holden's. Then he turned to me and did the last thing I expected.

He hugged me.

"Thank you," he whispered. "I forgot how daft she can be. If you ever need to talk about...well, I think you know...call me."

I felt a piece of paper slip into my hand, and I quickly pocketed it. "Anytime."

Beatrice showed him to the door herself, following him to wave him off. When she came back inside, she stared at me for a moment like she wanted to say something. Then, it passed and she made a show of parading us through the house toward the conservatory.

"We should go," Spencer whispered, pulling me closer to him as we went.

"Your brother is too drunk to drive. We have to take him with us."

"He could stay here."

"Is that a good idea?" I asked.

Spencer sighed like he'd just been handed a boulder to carry. "No, probably not. I'll talk to him. One drink and then we'll call it a night."

"Deal," I agreed. One drink couldn't hurt, could it?

12

The conservatory was nothing like the solarium at Sparrow Court. Spencer had turned that space into a greenhouse, cultivating exotic plants. This was nothing more than a climate-controlled glass room with a few potted plants and oversized lounge chairs. Nearby, a bar had been set up. Holden immediately prowled over to it and made himself comfortable.

"What's your poison?" he called over to me.

"I'm fine."

"Bollocks. I'm making you a drink." He began pouring and mixing as Spencer joined him. The two talked in low voices. Spencer kept his back to me, but I could see Holden's face as he made the cocktail, including every roll of his eyes.

"So, tell me." Beatrice plopped onto the chair next to me, lounging across it with her head propped on her hand. "How is he in bed?"

"Seriously?" I hissed. "Isn't that a little personal?"

"Please." She groaned and turned onto her back. "Don't be such a prude. You can't still be waiting for marriage. You had to do something to get that rock on your finger."

The shock of her words hit me square in the chest. Of course, Kerrigan probably was a virgin at Woldingham. She'd lost touch with Beatrice years ago.

"It's not like you haven't slept with Holden," I said, crossing my arms over my chest.

"Are you saying it's the same?" she asked. "Because that only inspires more questions—like how would you know? I mean, they are identical, but that doesn't mean they fuck the same. Or does it? Do you know?"

Her head lolled to the side and she stared at me, waiting for an answer.

"Of course, I don't know. I just..." But she'd cornered me. I felt trapped, certain that she would exact whatever calculated plans motivated her to reach out to me. The more time I spent with Beatrice, the less convinced I was that she was interested in reviving our friendship.

"Holden fucks like an animal," she said with a shrug. "Hard. Fast. Hard."

"You said that already," I pointed out, doing my best to sound uninterested in this information. But my memories kept returning to the sounds I'd heard in the loo at Hillgrove's.

"Trust me, it deserves two mentions." She pushed up, swinging her feet over the side. Lowering her voice, her eyes on the brothers still mixing drinks behind the bar. "Something tells me you'll find out sooner or later. Consider it an insider tip."

"I'm engaged to Spencer," I said coldly.

"You do you, babe. No judgment here." This time the look she gave them was positively primal. "Besides, who wouldn't take them both if they were offering?"

"Excuse me, I need the loo."

"Do you remember where it is?" she asked with saccharine-sweetness.

"Of course." I got up and headed back into the main house. I had no fucking clue where the loo was but I would rather wander aimless through Welbatten for eternity than show her even an ounce of weakness.

After twenty minutes, I understood what they meant when they said pride comes before the fall. Not only had I not located the bathroom, I also wasn't entirely certain where I'd wound up. There'd been no obvious loo on the main floor, so I'd dared to go upstairs. As soon as I made it up there, I found myself too afraid to open a door to actually do it. I was about to give up and hope I could handle another drink on an already full bladder, when Beatrice's butler appeared in the corridor.

"May I help you, Miss Belmond?" he asked quizzically.

"I was going to the loo. Beatrice told me to use hers," I lied, hoping it didn't sound too far fetched. "But honestly, it's been so long and I've had so much wine. I thought I remembered where it was, but I seem to be lost."

"Miss Highclere's quarters are the second on the left." He paused for a moment.

"Yes?" I asked.

He shifted uncomfortably. "It's not my place..."

"Oh, feel free." After dinner and then Beatrice's

inquest regarding my sex life, I could handle anything—and if the butler had caught me in a lie, I would rather know that now than find out through someone else later.

"It's nice to see one of Miss Highclere's friends grown up and acting like a mature young woman," he said in a rush.

I swallowed back a grin. Not because he'd flattered me, but because it was obvious that he found Beatrice as obnoxious as the rest of us did. "Thank you."

"Will you be able to find your way back?" he asked.

"I think so." It was more of a fib than a lie. I knew where the stairs were, from there, I just needed to go outside. Eventually, I'd reach the conservatory. I took my time in the loo, despite having been gone for such a long time already. I needed a break from it all. The double talk and keeping up appearances. Holden's meaningful looks and Spencer's guarded concern. And fucking Beatrice.

When I finally made it to the stairs, Spencer was on his way up them. He paused at the bottom.

"I thought you were lost."

"I just needed a few minutes. Too much wine at dinner."

"Too much Beatrice at dinner," he said, reaching for my hand when I hit the bottom stair. "I've been looking for you for a while. God knows what trouble Beatrice and Holden have gotten into in our absence."

"You left them alone?" I exhaled heavily as he steered us toward the back of the house. "Maybe we should just leave him. He obviously doesn't want to go."

"I wouldn't say that," Spencer explained. "He seems torn between getting in a shag and retreat."

"That's a masculine dilemma if I ever heard one," I grumbled. "Run from the woman or screw her."

We'd only made it out the back door when Spencer stopped in his tracks and grabbed my arm. "Wait."

"What?" I looked at him, trying to figure out what was wrong.

"It looks like we're interrupting something." He tipped his head toward the conservatory.

I took a step closer, unsure what he was talking about when I saw them. Without thinking, I took another step to get a better view. I couldn't quite believe what was happening, even as I watched Holden lift Beatrice off her feet and brace her against a glass wall. I was still staring when Spencer's arms slipped around my waist.

"Now this is an interesting predicament."

13

My breath hitched in my throat as Spencer's hands snaked up my body toward my breasts. He coaxed a few steps closer until we had the best possible viewing angle while still remaining hidden in the shadows. I couldn't tear my eyes away from the scene in front of me, even though Spencer was here and it felt wrong.

Because it was as though someone had lit every nerve in my body on fire. I couldn't look away, because I didn't want to. I was exactly what Holden claimed.

A dirty girl.

I needed to put a stop to this. Now.

But I didn't. Spencer plumped my breast over my blouse. Then unfastened a button to slide his hand under. His thumb and index finger found my nipple and began to knead it through my bra's lace. It pebbled into a rock hard point that sent me gasping, but still I watched Holden with Beatrice.

The unfortunate side effect of jumpsuits is that the whole thing has to come off if you want to shag. This was evidenced by the pile of sequined fabric lying a short distance from where Beatrice's naked body was pinned to the window. Her hands had pulled Holden's shirt up just enough to dig her nails into his back, but he hadn't bothered with removing his own clothes.

"Just like the loo at Hillgrove's," Spencer whispered as if he could read my thoughts. "You know I can't help wondering what you were doing while you listened to him fuck someone next to you." The words were hot against my ear. They tingled over my skin, finding their way to my core where they wound around the ache pulsing inside me and squeezed.

"I told you I was trying to stay quiet," I mumbled, resisting the urge to moan as he massaged my other breast.

Spencer's teeth nipped at my neck, stealing a sound of pleasure from me. Despite my intention to get things under control, I melted against him.

"Tell me what you did that day. I promise not to tell Holden." His raspy voice tempted me, but it was the sight of Holden's firm ass pumping tirelessly between Beatrice's legs that overcame my resistance.

"I touched myself," I confessed. I waited for the shame to come, but it didn't.

"Like this." He palmed my breast, and I shook my head.

One of his hands slipped to my trousers and unfastened them. "Show me, Kerrigan. Where did you touch yourself?"

My fingers trembled as I took his hand and guided it

between my legs. Before Spencer could dip them between my sex, I slid my own hand under his, taking the lead.

"Fuck, you're so hot," he grunted as I began to masturbate, his own hand covering mine as I worked my clit. "This is what you did?"

I nodded, my mouth dry and my eyes watching the two of them through the window. It was even hotter than the time at Hillgrove's because this time I could see it. Spencer pressed his hand harder against mine and began to move it, making the movements of my fingers harder. Rougher.

"Did you want to be the one in there? Losing your virginity instead of listening?" he asked as he increased his pace.

"Yes," I admitted. "I wanted to be fucked like that."

"Do you want to be fucked now—while you watch?" he asked gruffly.

I closed my eyes, wishing I could find any other answer than the one on my lips. "Please."

"You are so polite," he said with a dark chuckle. His hand slid free of mine. "Stop touching yourself. I want you to come on my cock."

I bit my lip as I withdrew my fingers. The pulse between my legs had grown to an unbearable, almost painful ache. "Please, Spencer," I cried softly. "Please fuck me."

He wrenched my pants downs and I gasped as the night air hit my warm, wet sex. A breeze tickled across it and I nearly came. Spencer's buckle clattered, followed by a zipping sound.

"Get on your hands and knees," he ordered.

There were possibly a million reasons to say no but none of them outweighed the arousal controlling my every decision. I lowered myself carefully to my knees then leaned forward until I was on all fours in front of him.

"Christ, Kerrigan," he slipped a finger inside me as he knelt down and I shuddered. "You're dripping. I think you're ready for me to fuck you. Are you?"

"Please fuck me," I repeated the request over and over, unsure if I was speaking aloud or locked inside my own head.

"You're not going to last long." His hands urged me open and then I felt the tip of his cock nudge against me. "So I'm going to fuck you until you come twice."

As if he'd seen the future, my body swelled as he slowly pushed inside me. The feeling started as a low fullness, an ache that seemed to grow within me. Time slowed, the pleasure seeping through me until my entire body felt that same delicious agony. I stopped breathing as though poison stole through my veins, and my only thought was what a wonderful way to die.

But right when total oblivion seemed within grasp, Spencer grabbed a handful of my hair and began to pound inside me. The out-of-body experience fractured. Small climaxes punctured my body, none fully allowing me to fall apart, but each drawing me closer and closer to a precipice.

"Are you watching them?" Spencer gritted out between thrusts.

My eyes turned to the conservatory as if commanded, and I mewled a "yes."

For a moment, I'd been so lost in my own body that I'd

forgotten what had initiated this moment. Holden. I saw him now with her. He'd flipped Beatrice around, pinning her body against the glass as he took her from behind like his brother did to me now. Reality crashed down on me and I felt dirt digging against my knees. My hands clutched fistfuls of grass for leverage. Spencer tugged at my hair, drawing my neck up.

"How about a better view?" He slammed into me hard. "I think she's about to come. See her legs. They're shaking. I want you to come with her."

I panted as his hold on my hair stretched my neck, allowing me a better view, but straining me for words and air. Not that I cared. My eyes went to Beatrice's slender legs, trembling and spread wide, so that Holden could piston inside her. Each time he thrust up, her feet left the floor. It was virile and punishing and the hottest thing I'd ever seen.

Spencer rocked into me, grunting, his own pace increasing to match his brother's. "Now."

I spilled over as I watched Beatrice contract and shake, my orgasm matching hers. But in the dark and secret cover of night, mine lingered, releasing wave after wave as I watched her sag against the glass, watched Holden withdraw and brush himself along her folds, watched him turn and pull up his pants. One last moan slipped from my mouth as he left her there, used and spent against the window to return to the bar.

Spencer stilled behind me, waiting a moment before he withdrew. He released my hair and a second later, I felt the lace of my underpants brush against my sore sex.

"Bit of a mess," he said in a tone rich with amusement as he cleaned me up. He helped me to my feet, pulling up his trousers before reaching for mine, still crumpled on the ground. He shook them, then eyed them thoughtfully. "I think they're okay, but these are soaked."

He balled my lace knickers up and shoved them in his pocket before he helped me finish dressing. He studied me, tucking an escaped strand of hair behind my ear. Something dark glinted in his eyes, impossible to hide even in the shadows. "Perfect. So perfect."

I ran my eyes along him, a strange but familiar sensation taking hold. Before he could see it on my face, I bent and brushed the knees of his trousers. I didn't know what to make of it. It was like deja vu. For a moment, I'd looked into the face of a stranger. When I straightened, I found Spencer waiting for me.

"Shall we?" he asked, crooking his arm.

I took it, slipping back to my place at his side. As we walked toward the conservatory, I saw that Beatrice had gotten dressed. Holden stood near the bar with a drink in his hand, his back turned away from her—from us. He didn't turn around when we entered. Beatrice glanced up, not a hair out of a place.

"I thought you two had gotten lost," she said with a knowing smile.

"We stopped to talk," Spencer said smoothly. "Drink?"

I nodded, not caring what he brought me as long as it was strong. He moved to join his brother at the bar and Beatrice patted the seat next to her.

"Join me."

I did as she asked, arranging myself carefully and wishing I'd gotten a chance to check my appearance in the mirror.

Beatrice leaned closer, speaking in a low voice. "I've been dying to get a minute alone with you."

"Me, too," I lied. Time alone with Beatrice was the last thing on my wishlist right under dying in a fiery plane crash and getting bit by a venomous snake.

"I have to say I'm surprised," she whispered.

I raised an eyebrow at the cryptic revelation. "About what?"

"You and Spencer." She shrugged. "Also, I hope you don't mind if I shag Holden."

I bit the inside of my cheek to keep myself from retorting. It was so magnanimous of her to ask after she already did that. "Why would I mind? Although, I thought you hated him."

"Oh, I do," she said, snorting slightly as if hatred was a silly objection instead of a hard limit. "But I guess you really are over him."

"Over him?" I blinked. Maybe it was the endorphins still flooding me, but I couldn't quite process what she was hinting at.

"Don't be coy." She giggled and batted my hand. "You two never hid it well, and remember, I caught you two kissing at Queen Charlotte's Ball or was it at the Royal Ascot. Nevermind, it hardly matters. I'm just glad to see you chose the right brother, Kerrigan."

She looked over her shoulder at the brothers, whose heads were bent together in quiet conversation. I couldn't think of a thing to say. Kerrigan and...Holden? It couldn't be true. Someone would have told me. Holden would have told me. He couldn't keep his mouth shut any other time. But, despite all the reasons Beatrice had to be wrong, I couldn't shake the feeling in my gut that she was telling me the truth.

But I hadn't picked. Kerrigan hadn't picked. We'd done as we were told, or, at least, I had. As I stared at the brothers, I couldn't help asking myself: if I was Kerrigan, which brother would be the right one?

14

"Kerrigan." Soft fingers brushed the side of my face, and I blinked, feeling fuzzy, to discover the room was dark.

"What time is it?" I croaked. It felt as though we'd just gotten home from Beatrice's dinner party moments ago. Sleep clung to my limbs, and I had to rub my eyes to get my brain to process the things coming out of Spencer's mouth.

"I should be back soon."

I sat up, realizing I missed a few important things. "What?"

"I guess you're actually awake now," he said dryly. Sighing, he launched into a repeat of whatever information he'd just delivered. "Grandfather took a fall. The doctors say he'll be fine, but mother is panicking and there are matters that need to be addressed."

"Now?" I fumbled for my watch on the nightstand and discovered it was four in the morning. "It can't wait until later?"

"Unfortunately not." He shook his head, placing a warm, strong hand on my bare shoulder. "It's just a few things. I hope to be back by nightfall."

I clutched the sheet to my chest. "Do you want me to come with you?"

It wasn't as though I relished the idea of hanging out at Hensley without him. I knew nothing about Yorkshire. My only friend here wasn't really my friend, at all. And this was supposed to be a romantic trip away.

"It will only take the day. You'll have much more fun here than waiting for me to take meetings and talk to doctors. You can go into the village or visit with Beatrice."

I fought the urge to grimace at the thought of spending time with her. Plus, there was another thing to consider. "I don't have a car. You're leaving me at the mercy of Holden."

Holden.

There it was: my reason to stay. I'd been avoiding Holden for weeks, but after what Beatrice told me last night, I finally had a clue as to why he was sure I was an imposter. But while that answered one question, it raised a dozen more.

"I would never do such a thing," Spencer reassured me. "I'm leaving the McLaren. The keys are on the desk."

"But how are you getting back to London?"

"Helicopter. It's arriving in a few minutes." He finished fastening a cufflink. "You're welcome to come along but I should be back by supper."

I frowned, not liking either choice very much. On one hand, I'd come here to spend time with Spencer but he was going to be somewhere else. The logical move to make was to go with him. But staying gave me access to Holden alone, making it easier to confront him. Of course, Holden was another good reason I should go. And there was the most important reason: it was four in the morning and I could barely keep my eyes open. I yawned, attempting to get some oxygen into my brain to help make a decision.

"You're staying," Spencer said. "Sleep all day if you like."

"But then I'll be up all night."

"You're going to be up all night anyway," Spencer promised. His hand moved to my chin and he leaned in to kiss me. "It's so hard to leave you."

"Then don't," I said, turning my lips down and pouting.

"I wish I could, but the helicopter will be out back soon."

"Wait," I said, something finally occuring to me through the fog, "do you have a helicopter pad?"

Spencer laughed and kissed me again. He stood and slowly released my hand. "Go back to sleep and dream of me."

"I will," I promised, settling back into bed and watching him disappear into the corridor. Spencer would be back soon, and for now, I would sleep. But when I drifted off, I dreamt of Holden.

If I didn't know better, I would have thought Holden knew I'd been dreaming about him. He greeted me on the veranda with a smirk, looking relaxed in a pair of worn jeans and a cable knit sweater.

"She lives," he said, pointing to a cup of coffee. I took the seat farthest from him and reached for the silver coffee pot. As I poured, I was relieved to see steam rising. It was still hot. I brought the cup to my lips, breathing in the rich aroma.

"It's only ten," I pointed out.

"Still, I was beginning to wonder if I should come up to kiss you," Holden said.

I snapped out of my trance, my heart beginning to pound. "Why would you do that?"

"Isn't that how the story goes? The prince goes to the sleeping beauty and wakes her with a kiss?"

"I'm not sleeping beauty," I muttered and turned my attention to my coffee, hoping he didn't see the cup trembling. There was absolutely no way that Holden knew I'd been dreaming of him doing just that—and more—before I'd finally woken up this morning.

"You're grouchy in the mornings," he commented. "Are you warm enough? It's a bit chilly this morning."

"I'm fine." I did my best to sound indifferent. The truth was that it wasn't the cooler, autumnal air pinkening my cheeks, it was the flush of embarrassment. Less than a half hour ago, I'd been dreaming that Holden had me up against a window, his lips on mine, as we gave in to each other. I'd said his name over and over in the dream, thoroughly erasing any hope that I'd been dreaming of Spencer.

Neither of them needed to know that.

"Where is Spencer anyway?" Holden asked.

"He didn't tell you," I said, a little surprised, even though Spencer had left so early in the morning.

"Tell me what?" Holden was suddenly curious.

I picked up a piece of toast and began slathering it with butter, doing my best to avoid his eyes. "Your grandfather fell. Nothing serious," I added quickly, "but Spencer went back to take care of a few things."

"Family things or business things?" Holden asked quietly.

Although I'd been doing my best to not meet his eyes, something in his tone lifted my gaze to him now. Holden's face was a mask of stony detachment, but I knew what I'd heard hiding in his voice: hurt. "I really couldn't say. I'm sure that it was something to do with Parliament."

That seemed like the right excuse to give him. Anything with Parliament, Spencer would handle. However, Holden merely shrugged, almost instantly adopting a devil-may-care attitude. "At least, I didn't have to go all the way home to London to be useless. How long will Spencer be gone?"

"He said he'll be back this evening." I swallowed the bite of toast I'd been chewing, suddenly finding my throat was dry. It scratched on the way down, but that discomfort was nothing to the wicked gaze Holden pinned on me now. "What? Why are you staring at me?"

"I finally got you alone, dirty girl."

A bit of my dream flashed to mind, and I shook my brain. I needed to keep control of this situation. "Holden, I —"

"We need to talk," he cut me off.

"About what?" I did my best to sound innocent and turned my attention to a platter of scones. Getting abandoned by Spencer was one thing. Being left with Holden called for carbs to distract me. I picked one up and put it back down in favor of another. But even as I tried to act naturally, I felt him watching me.

"Is that how you want to play it?" he asked.

"I really have no idea what you're talking about." I managed to keep my voice even despite how my heart was hammering in my chest. I wasn't sure how long I would be able to keep things under control. Just then, as if my body had decided for me, black spots moved into the corners of my vision. The rest of my body grew heavy like it was being dragged down, falling apart like Holden had planned.

"Not now," I moaned to myself.

"We have to talk about it."

But I wasn't speaking to Holden. I continued muttering, abandoning the scone, to press my fingers to my forehead. My eyes slammed shut, fighting the oncoming panic attack. But it was strong—stronger than any I've had for weeks—and I felt myself slipping away. I threw a hand out to steady myself against the table, afraid I might fall out of my chair and tried to coach myself through, muttering, "Not now. Not Fucking now."

"Are you okay?" Holden's voice was distant and concerned. There was a rustle of fabric, and, a moment later, he was kneeling beside my chair. A strong hand landed on my back as if he, too, suspected I was on the verge of fainting. "Do you need a doctor?"

I shook my head so fast that I swayed in my seat. Stars joined the black spots in my vision, making the world feel like a might had fallen. It called to me — the darkness — and I knew I wouldn't avoid it much longer.

"Kerrigan!" Holden yelled.

"Not my name," I muttered, dimly aware that we both knew the truth. "Not my name."

"Fuck, I know that. But since I don't know what to call you..." Holden's frustration fizzled out before it exploded. "Let's get you inside."

I dipped in and out of consciousness, so I didn't realize what was happening until Holden stood and scooped me into his arms. Somewhere a voice in the back of my mind screamed in protest, and I reached out a hand to smack him. I shouldn't be in his arms. He shouldn't be the one taking care of me. But I found myself clinging to him instead. Somehow, Holden had become my last grasp on reality.

Well, I was screwed.

Holden carried me into the house. I had no idea where he was taking me until he started up the stairs.

"Oh no," I mumbled. "Not to bed."

He chuckled, sounding bemused. "Keep your knickers on, dirty girl. I'm only taking you to lie down."

Holden kept his word. He carried me to the room I shared with Spencer and placed me on the bed. Since I'd gone down to breakfast, someone on the staff had already made it up. Holden arranged pillows around me, then took a seat at my side.

"Just breathe," he coaxed me.

Fingers wove through mine and I latched on — to him, to the world, to now. I did as he suggested focusing everything on my breathing.

In.

Out.

In.

Out.

Gradually, the fuzzy sensation in my brain began to fade. After another minute, I dared to crack my eyelids open a fraction. Holden's worried face stared back at me. As the panic attack subsided, the world came rushing back. The room was quiet except for our breathing. Sun streamed through the window, creating a warm pool of light on the bed. I blinked to allow my eyes to adjust, and as I did every nerve in my body zeroed in on my hand. My hand was still clasped with Holden's. His thumb rubbed circles on the back of it. His grip was warm and firm and for a moment — for the first time in a long time — every ounce of fear vanished from me.

"I'm sorry. I —"

"Shh," Holden hushed me. "Take a minute. There's no rush."

I allowed myself to linger with him, hand in hand, telling myself that I was just following his instructions. But the truth was much messier.

After a minute, I drew my hand away from his. Holden glanced down at his empty palm, a shadow flashing across his face, before he mustered a smirk.

"Want to tell me what that was, dirty girl?" He didn't move from the bed.

"Panic attack," I said in a clipped tone. "It happens sometimes." The last thing I needed was Holden to have more dirt on me—or for him to care.

"Sometimes?" he stressed. "How often?"

"Just every once in a while. It's no big deal," I added. I started to push myself up on the bed. Somewhere, not so deep inside me, I knew that being alone with Holden, in a room, on a bed, was a wildly bad idea.

But Holden held out a hand to stop me. "What do you think you're doing?"

"Getting up," I snapped back.

"Is it that bad to be around me?" he asked, catching me off guard as the cockiness on his face softened.

"It's just that I don't want anyone to get the wrong idea." Least of all, me.

"Just give yourself a minute. If you want me to go, I will. I just want to know that you are okay." Resignation slumped his shoulders, and he stood to leave.

I watched as he turned toward the door. There were

one million reasons to let him walk away. Ten million, actually. But for some reason, I called, "Stop."

Holden swiveled to face me, but he didn't return to the bed. Instead, he prowled to the chaise lounge and sank down on its seat. "I'll stay over here."

"That's a good idea," I agreed.

"Why is that, dirty girl? Afraid you won't be able to keep your hands off me?" He lounged back on the chaise, throwing an arm across its sloped back.

"That's not it," I said in a fluster. "If someone sees us in here, it would be best if we weren't on the bed together."

"Whatever you need to tell yourself." He shot me a wolfish grin that made my stomach flip.

It was time to set some ground rules—for both our sakes. "You know, if you're just going to shamelessly flirt with me, you can leave."

"Me? Shameless?" He pretended to look hurt by clutching his chest.

"I suspect if I googled shameless, your face appears," I said dryly.

"All right, dirty girl, we'll do things your way. No flirting—shameless or otherwise."

"That's a start." I nodded, relieved that he wasn't going to fight me on it. "But how do I know I can trust you?"

"That's easy." He shrugged his broad shoulders and penned a piercing look on me. "Because I've kept your secret this long."

My heart began to pound again, beating inside me like a trapped prisoner desperate to escape. "What secret?"

"Okay, I won't shamelessly flirt with you, but you have to stop acting like I'm an idiot."

"I'm not acting like you're an idiot," I said defensively. "I'm just not sure—"

"I know." He didn't need to clarify what he knew. The truth was written across his face. "I might not know everything, but I know you're not Kerrigan Belmond. So, do me the courtesy of not acting like I'm stupid."

I paused, considering what my next move was. Part of me wanted to double down and convince him that he was mistaken. But I knew that was a desperate and ill-conceived play. Holden knew the truth. I could continue to deny it, or I could see exactly what he planned to do with the information.

I made my choice. "Shut the door."

A smile as slow as honey spread over his lips, but the moment he opened his mouth, he shut it again. Instead, he went to the door and closed it quietly. The whole while looking like it was physically difficult to not say something.

"That looked painful, but I'm proud of you for not shamelessly flirting," I told him, relaxing a little into the pillows again.

"I'll be cured in no time," he said with a snort.

It was counterintuitive to feel safer with Holden behind closed doors, but I did. Leaving it open, meant that anyone could hear something as they passed. We would have to be careful later, so that no one saw us leaving the bedroom together, but for the first time I felt I could be myself with him. No one was watching. No one could hear. And he already knew the truth.

It was actually a relief.

"What's your name?" he began as he resumed his seat on the lounger.

"Kate," I told him. I felt a weight lifted from my shoulders as I said my name.

"Nice to meet you, Kate," he said. "Are you seeing anyone?"

"Holden," I said in a warning voice. He'd made it less than a minute without flirting.

He raised his hands in surrender. "That's a genuine question. I'm curious about who you are."

"You know who I am," I said.

"Not really. You're claiming to be Kerrigan Belmond. You look just like her, by the way, so you're nailing it," he said in an oddly complimentary tone.

I hesitated. "Thank you?"

"Yeah, I don't know how to feel about it either," he admitted. "You're living in her house. You're engaged to my brother as her. You've slept with him. How far are you going to take this thing?"

Within thirty seconds, he'd managed to get to the heart of what plagued my every waking moment. "Just until she comes back."

"What? I don't understand."

"Kerrigan is traveling. I'm just pretending to be her until she comes home," I explained. "It's all part of an arrangement."

"So, you're not some con artist?"

"Con artist?" I choked on the word. Is that what he

thought of me? "No, Todd Belmond found me and asked me to do this."

Holden's eyes widened in surprise like this had never occurred to him. "And you said yes? What, were you bored or something?"

"Not that it's any of your business, but it's a job." I crossed my arms over my chest, refusing to feel guilty for thinking about myself and my own future. I had made my choice. People like Holden never had to worry about paying rent or electric bills. They never went hungry because the money had run out. He couldn't understand.

"You're getting paid?"

"I know you don't have much experience with these things," I began flatly, "but that's usually how a job works."

"So Kate is a class warrior," he said in an amused voice.

"Kate isn't anything. I just wasn't sure if you have any idea how the real world works."

"Oh, I know, dirty girl." His eyes narrowed, all friendliness vanishing from his face. "Do you?"

"I think I'm doing okay so far."

He laughed. "Why? Because you look like some rich guy's daughter? That's not taking care of yourself, that's luck."

"Sometimes luck is seeing opportunity for what it is." I shrugged. I'd seized a chance at a better life. I wouldn't let him make me feel badly for that.

"Look, I'm not judging you. I hope that you squeeze every cent you can out of him. And my brother, for that matter. I just wanted you to admit the truth," he confessed.

"Is that really why?" I felt bolder now that the lie was no longer between us. "Or is there another reason?"

"What are you implying, Kate?" He clicked his tongue against his teeth as he said my name.

But he could nip at me all he wanted. He wouldn't get a bite. "I figured out how you knew I wasn't Kerrigan. I should have realized sooner." I paused. "You two had a thing."

I waited for him to challenge me, but he didn't. "Yeah, we had a thing."

His jaw tensed and he shook his head in disgust, leaving me to wonder what about his past with Kerrigan had left him looking so angry.

"So you knew the whole time?" I asked.

"That you weren't Kerrigan? I figured it out pretty quickly. At first, I thought you were being a bitch and ignoring me," he said unapologetically. "And then I realized you really didn't know who I was — and that was, well, impossible."

"Why? Because you're so memorable"? I rolled my eyes.

But when they found him again, his were blazing. "No," he answered in a thick voice, "because Kerrigan and I were in love with each other."

16

I hadn't seen Holden since that morning. I wondered if he was avoiding me, too. There was plenty of space to hide in Hensley House, but somehow it still felt too small—too claustrophobic—still. Every corner I turned, every corridor I roamed, I expected to find him. But I didn't. After a while, the anxiety of running into him became too much for me. I needed to clear my head before I saw him again.

I couldn't seem to do that in the massive country estate.

Spencer's keys were still on the nightstand. I found a jacket in the wardrobe and decided to follow his advice. I'd go into the village or drive around. Maybe space would help me figure out what to do. I'd never driven a car as expensive as the McLaren. It took me a moment to find all of its bells and whistles, but try as I might, I couldn't figure out how to work the navigation. I'd never find the village without it. It hardly mattered, though. I didn't really care about the village. I just needed to get away from here.

The Yorkshire countryside was beautiful in early autumn. The turning leaves dusted the roadways with jeweled petals that seemed brighter in the day's gloomy light. Clouds hung over the moors. I drove aimlessly, turning down lanes on a whim and ignoring road signs.

I tapped the leather-wrapped steering wheel and wondered how much longer I could hold up my end of my arrangement with Tod Belmond. Holden's revelation left me to wonder if that was why she had run away. He hadn't given me any more details. I had no idea how long ago they'd been involved. Maybe the idea of facing Holden while agreeing to marry his brother was too much for her to bear. But even if that was the case, it didn't explain where she was now. Something wasn't right about Tod Belmond and his obsession with seeing this marriage through. When I first met him, I'd written it off as some ridiculous, rich person thing. Arranged marriages? Just another quirk of the aristocracy. Now I was beginning to wonder what secrets he was keeping. And if he was hiding things, could I trust Giles or Iris?

I wanted to. God, I wanted to trust them.

I slowed the car as I came to a gate at the end of a country lane. Sheep milled about, their wool was thick and wiry as if they were preparing for the coming winter. How long before someone came to shear them to make expensive sweaters? I put the car in reverse, but paused and watched them run. They divided as if clearing a path, and a moment later, a dog raced through them. Then, a man appeared in thick tweed and tall boots. He waved to me, unperturbed to find a woman sitting near his gate watching his flock. I could hear their bleating cries through the windows. But they didn't run from the shepherd once he stood among them. They didn't run from the man fattening them. They didn't flee from the one who would steal their coats. They didn't know any better.

That's what dependence did. It built false trust. It led lambs to slaughter.

I had jumped at the chance to leave London and all those questions I couldn't bear to ask. I couldn't do that much longer. Not with the wedding date set for December. Not without knowing where Kerrigan was and if her father had contact with her. I'd allowed myself to be bought. I allowed myself to follow him like these lambs followed their shepherd. How many of them were going to slaughter? Was that where Tod was leading me?

And none of that told me what to do about Holden.

He hadn't asked for my cooperation. He didn't try to blackmail me. But it was only a matter of time. I knew that. There was no way he would keep silent about who I really was without something in return. But the worst part of it—the thing I couldn't escape no matter how far I drove—was that deep inside me, I wanted to be in his debt.

I could never have Spencer. Even if Tod Belmond expected me to go through with the wedding, I wouldn't be able to lie to him forever. Not while it was getting harder and harder to maintain the line between my life and hers. Marrying Spencer, even temporarily in her name, might make it impossible for me to remember who I was. No, I couldn't have Spencer. Not much longer anyway. Once he knew the truth, he would hate me.

But Holden saw me. He knew. I could be myself around him. At least, I thought so. I'd wanted him from the moment we met. But even that couldn't last. I was living a borrowed life. I was walking in another woman's shoes. Sooner or later, I had to find my own pair.

I continued down the lane, pausing at the end with no clue which way to turn. Not only because I had no idea where I was, but also because I had no place in this world. I didn't know what direction I was heading. I didn't know where I would land two months from now or a year or even tomorrow. I couldn't return to the woman I was only months ago. I wasn't sure I could even return to the woman I was this morning.

Taking out my mobile, I dialed Eliza, hoping she wasn't at work. It didn't ring but went straight to voicemail.

"Hey girl, just checking in," I said as the first tears swelled up my throat. I swallowed hard, forcing my voice to stay even as I continued, "Just give me a call back."

I hung up before I broke down. The last thing I wanted was for Eliza to worry about me.

I just wanted someone to talk to, but I had no one. No friends. No one I could confide in or ask for help.

And then a completely mental, but possibly brilliant, thought occurred to me. Reaching for my bag, I dug around until I found the scrap of paper from the night before. I stared at the number for a moment, wondering if I could trust him. In the end, I decided that a man with his family was probably pretty good at keeping secrets. At least, I hoped he was.

. . . .

Edward met me at the end of the drive to Harewood House. He waved as I parked the McLaren and turned off the engine. A charming smile overtook his handsome face. He was good-looking in a boyish way. There was something of perpetual youth about him. Maybe it was his curly black hair or the sparkle in his eyes that tragedy hadn't dimmed. But there was something about him that made him feel like a friend.

"You called," he said, coming to help me out of the car.

"I hope that's okay." I bit my lip. It'd taken more than a little courage to actually dial his number. He was royalty, after all. But not only had he invited me over straight away, he'd even helped me figure out how to use the bloody navigation in the McLaren so I could figure out where I was.

"I'm glad you didn't get lost." Our feet crunched along the rocky drive as we made our way to the house.

"I think it took me twice as long as it should," I confessed with a laugh. "That's what I get for driving around in a place I don't know."

Edward tilted his head, confusion clouding his eyes. "I thought you'd been to Yorkshire before. Beatrice mentioned you two used to come up here when you were in school."

"Yes," I said quickly, searching for a way to cover my error. "I just never drove then. It's funny how strange a place feels when you're the one in charge."

"I can't say I know," Edward said grimly.

"Oh, I'm sorry." I wasn't entirely certain what I had said, but he waved off my apology.

"It's nothing. Welcome to Harewood."

I thought Welbatten and Hensley were impressive, but I'd

never stepped foot into a royal residence before. Harewood was a Jacobean masterpiece. Ivy clung to the brick walls in thick patches that draped romantically over leaded windows. I spied beautiful gardens around the side of the estate. Edward led me inside where I found myself momentarily struck dumb. I'd seen plenty of art collections between the Belmonds and the Byrds. Even Beatrice's family seemed to have quite the collection. None of them matched what hung in just the entry of Harewood. Within a moment I had spotted a Renoir, a Monet, a Hogarth, and a Waterhouse. The foyer could be a museum.

"Your house is magnificent," I said breathlessly.

"We have centuries of imperialism to thank for it," he said dryly. He pointed to a sitting room. "Should we stay inside or would you rather speak more privately?"

There was no sign that anyone but Edward was here, but I knew better. An estate as large as Harewood, owned by the royal family, probably had a small army of people working inside and out.

"Private would be better." I didn't plan to tell him everything, but I didn't want to run the risk of someone overhearing. That was how gossip got started.

"I know just where we can go."

We chatted about Yorkshire and other trivial topics as we made our way out the rear entrance of the house. Edward guided me past a number of hedges and manicured gardens down a paved path until we came to a wrought iron arch covered in more ivy.

"This is my favorite part of this property," he explained as we passed the arch. As soon as we were through, I understood why. A courtyard, surrounded on all sides by tall hedges was broken by what appeared to be a shallow, stone staircase that led to nowhere. But it wasn't a staircase. Water trickled down the steps until it reached a pool. Lily pads floated on its surface and I caught glimpses of coy darting around the roots.

"It's so peaceful," I breathed.

"That's why I love it." He sounded pleased. "I figured you might need a little peace in your life right now."

"Is it that obvious?"

He laughed, but it felt flat on my ears, lacking real amusement but containing plenty of sympathy. "Your life seems complicated."

"It's not supposed to be," I said quietly. "Everything's being planned for me. There shouldn't be any complications when it's all being handled."

"Tell me about it." He shoved his hands in his pockets and gave me a sympathetic smile. "If I'm not being too bold, can I ask you a personal question?"

"Ask away, your highness."

"Please don't call me that," he said darkly. "I'd rather not be reminded of my title here."

I nodded, murmuring an apology. It seemed that Edwards' life was as complicated as mine, at the moment.

"You can ask me anything," I said.

"Was the engagement between you and Spencer arranged?"

"Yes, but we really do care for each other."

"I picked up on that," he said quickly. "But Beatrice

mentioned that it was and then, there seemed to be some tension between you and Holden."

"We have history," I told him. I didn't go into details, because I didn't have any. But somehow it felt pertinent that Kerrigan and Holden had a relationship, even if it wasn't mine to claim.

He grimaced. "That does complicate things. But it's over?"

"I thought it was." I wandered around the pool, trying to spot the goldfish in the water. But they hid from me. "I'm not sure what I'm supposed to do."

"I'm probably not the best person to give romantic advice," he admitted. "I haven't been very lucky in love myself." The bitter edge of his words made my heart hurt for him, and before I could think better of it, I reached over and took his hand.

"How are you doing?" I asked. He stared at me for a moment and I realized how presumptuous I was being. Edward was kind, but we weren't really friends. I dropped his hand quickly and shook my head. "I'm sorry. I shouldn't have pried into your personal life."

"No, it's fine." He took my hand again and squeezed it. "Everyone does it. I just get the impression none of them really care."

"What do you mean?"

"Everyone's just going through the motions. No one knows what to think. David betrayed—" he cut himself off quickly.

"You?" I guessed. "You don't have to talk about this."

"There are just things about his death that nobody

knows. I can't talk about them." He gave me a tight smile. "But now that he's gone, I wonder if I knew him at all."

"Why would you worry about that?" It was common knowledge that David had died as part of the plot against the monarchy. No one knew much more about what had happened, and the royal family had kept quiet about the details. It had been a scandal when Edward married. Now that his husband was gone, the press seemed even more interested in digging up dirt. I wondered what Edward had found in the process.

"It's hard to explain. Once someone is gone and you're left with all the pieces of their life, you start to put those pieces together. I guess you want to recreate them like they are a puzzle that can be rebuilt," he said slowly. "But sometimes the picture that starts to form isn't how you remember them."

I listened without speaking. It wasn't entirely the same, but I understood what he was saying. I was trying to do the same thing, trying to figure out who Kerrigan Belmond was. I was trying to piece together her life with what she had left behind. But no matter how hard I tried, the picture seemed all wrong.

"I think I know what you mean," I told him. "That must be hard. Is that why you're in Yorkshire?"

"I just wanted to be alone." He stared out on the land surrounding us, looking to some distant place I couldn't see. "Maybe I'm hiding. Everyone in my life is happy and in love. They're having babies and lives and...."

"It makes you think of what you lost," I finished for him, and he nodded.

"I know I can't run away forever, but I just need more time." He paused and then smiled shyly. "But you didn't come here to hear my sad story. So, what are you going to do about having two gorgeous brothers in love with you?"

"I don't know if either of them are in love with me," I said dismissively.

"I saw them last night. Trust me. They're both in love with you."

Neither had said it. Spencer had hinted at it, but the words had yet to cross his lips

"Sometimes I wish I didn't have to choose," I confessed to him.

His eyebrow arched and the smile on his face turned into a smirk. "Now that would shake up the aristocracy."

I blinked, wondering what he meant. Then I realized what it sounded like. A furious blush painted my cheeks and I shook my head. "That's not what I meant! I just meant that I don't know if I'm ready to get married."

And that was really the truth. I'd been asked to pretend to be Kerrigan Belmond. Tasked to stand in for her while she took an extended holiday. I had never expected to be put in the position to make choices that could define her whole life.

"Sorry. Although, I wouldn't blame you if you wanted both of them to yourself."

"The thought has occurred to me," I whispered, and we both laughed.

"You'd be crazy if it didn't," he agreed. "If you're not ready to get married, then don't."

He made it sound so simple. If only he knew how twisted my world was becoming.

"Can I ask you a personal question?"

He nodded. "Anything."

I swallowed and tried to think of the most delicate way to phrase it. "How did you know you were ready to get married?"

"I didn't," he said sheepishly. His face darkened for a moment. "I knew that David wanted to. At least, I thought he did."

"And that's why you married him?"

"It was important to him." He shrugged his shoulders, but sadness echoed in his words. "Love isn't always about what you want. Not when it's real. When it's real, sometimes it's about what they want."

17

Hensley was quiet when I returned that evening. I'd managed to make it back despite two wrong turns. I stopped in the doorway and took off my jacket, hoping I could find some food in the kitchen. I hated the idea of putting anyone out. But before I could make my way to check, Holden appeared on the stairs, freezing when he saw me.

There was a moment of tension, and then he exploded. "Where the fuck have you been?"

My mouth fell open, but I quickly shut it. Mustering up a glare, I planted a hand on my hip as if daring him to ask again. "That's none of your business."

"Like hell, it's not. Spencer has been trying to reach you for hours. I even drove around looking for you." His fingers curled around the wooden bannister. "I was worried. Really fucking worried."

I balked at this revelation. Holden worried? But that's what he had said. *I was worried.* Not we were worried. *I* was worried. It took me a minute to gather my scrambled thoughts. "I just went for a drive."

"You shouldn't be driving," he announced.

"Spencer left me his car. It's fine with him."

Holden released the railing and came down the stairs. "Does he know about your panic attacks?"

Was that what this was about? "Look, they don't happen that often. There's no reason I can't drive."

"I'll take that as a no." A muscle ticked in his jaw as he stepped into the light from the overhead chandelier. Everything about him was on edge. Muscles rippled with tension under his shirt. His shoulders were squared as if bracing for an attack. Shadows lingered on his face. But his eyes were another story.

They were full of a different emotion: relief.

"I'm sorry. I wasn't thinking. I should have left a note."

"You should have answered your phone," he said through gritted teeth.

"I was with a friend." I pulled my phone out of my bag and checked it. There were three missed calls from Spencer. And a dozen from Holden. "I'm sorry. I didn't realize I'd put it on silent."

"What friend?" he asked, ignoring my apology. "I called Beatrice."

"Were you checking up on me?" I asked, annoyance beginning to take root.

"I was trying to find you. For all I knew, you'd blacked out and run off the road. Hit a tree or wound up in a pond. You could have gone off a cliff."

"Are there a lot of cliffs one might accidentally drive off around here?" I asked dryly.

"It's not funny. I've been looking for hours."

Hours? "Does Spencer need to talk to me that badly?"

Holden glowered, his eyes narrowing. "How should I know? I'm not your messenger. I'm not even worthy of a quick note."

He stomped off towards the kitchen, leaving me there in stunned silence. I put my bag on a table near the door and took a deep breath. One problem at a time.

I dialed Spencer. When he picked up, I blurted out, "So sorry. My ringer was off."

"It's not a big deal," he said slowly.

"Holden said you were trying to reach me."

"I was, but I left a message with him. Did he give it to you?"

I looked to where Holden had disappeared down the hall and sighed. "No. We aren't really speaking."

"That didn't take long," Spencer laughed. "Look, I hate to do this, but I have to stay the night. They've called an emergency session of Parliament and my grandfather needs my help. I'm hoping to leave tomorrow night."

"Oh." I closed my eyes and slumped against the door.

"Kerrigan?" he pressed after a moment of silence. "I'm really sorry. If you want to drive back, I understand."

I could only imagine what his brother would have to say about that. Plus, there was the very real possibility that I would miss a turn and wind up in Wales.

"Tomorrow?" I said instead. "I can wait."

"Thursday at the latest," he promised but his words felt empty.

"Of course. Don't worry about me. I'll be fine. I love it here." That was somewhat true. I thought Yorkshire was beautiful. Besides, Kerrigan would never dream of standing between her fiancé and important matters of state. That was the whole point of her existence.

To be the perfect wife standing beside the perfect candidate for Prime Minister when the day came.

"Wonderful. I'll let you know as soon as I'm on my way back. And Kerrigan..." He paused and my heart jumped into my throat. "I miss you."

It plummeted back into place. "I miss you, too."

We hung up, leaving me to feel foolish and silly. Of course, he wasn't going to say I love you and even if he was, did I really want to hear it?

It was just my luck that Parliament would be called into an unexpected session the week my ambitious boyfriend had driven me five hours away to the north. I hoped Spencer was right and the meeting would be brief. That only meant dealing with Holden's volatile mood swings and shameless flirting for another day. I didn't dare consider how I would handle it if the session went longer.

Being stuck at Hensley left me two choices: I could avoid Holden or I could patch things up.

I thought of my conversation with Edward earlier. Things were complicated between us, because I didn't know who Holden was and what he meant to Kerrigan. But also because he had information that could destroy the arrangement I'd made with Tod Belmond. I didn't really have a choice at all.

I found Holden in the kitchen standing in the dark. I moved closer and discovered he was digging into the chocolate pudding that Spencer had introduced me to. My stomach growled and he looked up.

"Maybe you should see a doctor about that. I've never heard a human being make that noise," he informed me and turned back to the dessert.

It took me a moment to locate the flatware. When I finally did, I grabbed a spoon. "Share?"

"I don't suppose I have a choice." He eyed me. "I'm scared of what will happen if I refuse."

I rolled my eyes. "I'm not going to faint."

"I was more concerned about you eating me. Judging from the noise you make—" he pointed to my belly "—you might be part bear."

"You're hilarious." I bumped him over with my hip and dug my spoon into the chocolate. Taking my first bite, I sighed with pleasure. When I glanced over at Holden, he was watching me.

He looked away, but I caught the slide of his throat, as he spooned another bite. "Everything okay with Spencer?"

"He's stuck in London. He said he left a message with you."

"Yeah, well, he didn't tell me why he was staying," he said bitterly.

"Emergency session of Parliament," I informed him. "Your grandfather needs his help."

"Naturally." Holden fell silent. We continued to eat

until we'd put a sizable, and slightly embarrassing, dent in the pudding.

"Look," I said when I'd finally gathered my courage, "I am sorry that I worried you."

He tipped his head. "If you want to go to the village or to visit *this friend* of yours, I'll drive you."

"Holden, you don't have—"

"Yeah, I do." He turned his face toward mine. Even in the dark room, I saw the pained frustration in his eyes. "Don't fight me on this. You shouldn't be driving if you're having attacks like that."

There was no point in arguing with him, so I simply agreed. "Fine. But I doubt I'll be visiting my friend anytime soon."

"Do I know this friend of yours?"

"I went to see Edward," I said casually.

Holden's spoon paused over the dish. "You're really climbing the social ladder, aren't you, Kate?"

"It's not like that." His dig stung. Maybe it looked that way to him. Now that he knew I was a poor, uneducated stand-in, he obviously thought I was nobody. "I just wanted to see a friendly face."

"My face isn't friendly?" he murmured. "I thought you rather liked it."

"No shameless flirting," I reminded him.

"That was earlier. It wasn't a permanent arrangement."

What a surprise. "Holden, just tell me what you're planning to do."

"Planning?"

"You know I'm not Kerrigan." I couldn't believe he was

going to force me to admit it again. "So, when are you going to tell your brother?"

"Is that what you are worrying about?" he asked.

"I need time to talk to Tod and warn him that his plan isn't going to work." I kept my explanation matter-of-fact, choosing to ignore the pit growing in my stomach. Only a few days ago, I had been worried about December wedding plans. Now, I didn't even have that long. "And to figure out where I'm going to go."

He laid his spoon on the counter and turned to face me directly. "Where were you before?"

"Waiting tables at a pub in West Bexby." I shrugged and took another bite, but the chocolate tasted like dirt in my mouth. I tossed my spoon on top of his and pushed the plate away.

"Where the fuck is West Bexby?"

"Exactly," I said with a sigh. "I can call my flatmate. Hopefully, they haven't hired anyone. Although, I was a shit waitress, so maybe Lou won't even want me back."

He studied me for a moment, his features too shadowed for me to get a read on what he was thinking. Could he tell what I was thinking or was he just as in the dark as I was? "Something tells me you were a shit waitress."

"Thanks," I bit out. "But I've got to do something. Not all of us were born with a silver spoon in our mouths."

"Ouch," he said flatly. "Is that what you think of me?"

I lounged against the counter on my elbows, staring at the clock on the microwave oven. It was getting late. "Maybe."

"Is that what you think about Spencer?"

"Why would I feel differently about him?" I asked.

"I thought that was our entire problem: you feeling differently about me." He took a step closer and the sleeve of his sweater brushed my arm.

Tiny sparks crackled over my skin as if my body sensed his nearness. I shifted away from him. Nothing good could come of too much contact with Holden. "What are you going to tell him?"

"That's difficult." Holden took a deep breath as if he hadn't quite decided. "Perhaps, we can reach an arrangement?"

"What do you want?" My fingers gripped the edge of the counter, and I braced myself for his demand. I'd barely managed to get the question out of my mouth before it went dry. This was what I'd expected since he'd called me out that night. I'd known it was coming. But I didn't feel angry or afraid, just a little nervous and under that something that felt dangerously like excitement.

"You want me to keep this—and I'm just going to say it—*ludicrous* plan from my brother."

"He'll know eventually or..."

"Or?" he prompted with obvious interest.

"Kerrigan will return, and it won't matter," I said simply. Nothing about the plan had really changed other than the time table and the slight hitch of Holden knowing the truth.

"Is that what you think? She'll just come back and do what her daddy tells her?" Holden shook his head in disgust.

"I don't care what she does. That's her problem."

"But you don't care what mess you make of her life until then," he accused.

"Is that what you think?" The storm inside me broke free and I whirled to him. I jabbed a finger into his hard chest. "All I do is worry about fucking things up for some woman I've never even met! You can be self-righteous if you want. But don't judge me for taking the chance someone dropped in my lap! You've never been hungry. You've never worried about if you'll have a roof over your head that night. And you sure as hell have never wondered why you were even born!"

There was a pause. But if I thought Holden was digesting my tirade I was wrong, because a moment later he laughed. It was flat and harsh, sounding more like a bark than amusement. "Is that so, dirty girl? You told me your secret, so let me tell you one of mine."

"I don't give a fuck about your secrets. Do whatever you want, Holden. You're going to anyway." I pivoted toward the door but he grabbed my wrist.

"Yes, I'm rich. Yes, my life looks perfect. But you're wrong about one thing. I have spent ninety percent of my life wishing I'd never been born." He loosened his grip on me. "So, I guess we have that in common."

But he wasn't going to trick me into feeling sorry for him. "Poor little rich bastard," I spat back. "What did you do for the other ten percent: fuck everything that moves?"

"You really want to know? The other ten percent I was with her," he murmured, catching me off guard. He dropped my wrist and turned away from me. "Go ahead and laugh."

But I didn't, because it wasn't funny. Not at all. Shame washed over me like a sudden downpour, cold and unwelcome. I don't know why I felt guilty for what I said, but I did all the same.

We stood there in total silence. We'd finally shown our cards, but neither of us were holding the hands we thought. He had really loved her. I no longer doubted that. I just didn't know what he planned to do about it—or me.

"I'm not going to tell Spencer." His announcement cracked the silence. "On one condition."

I swallowed. I'd agreed to this charade, knowing there would be consequences. I couldn't escape them now nor would I try. I still owed it to myself to think about my own interests. I was the only one who would. "What do you want?"

"One day."

"Of what?" I asked in a strained voice. "Sex?"

This time he chuckled. "For twenty-four hours we do whatever I want. My rules. My way. Take it or leave it."

"Take it," I said through gritted teeth. It wasn't like I had a choice.

18

____

Holden's clock began the moment I said yes, so I was surprised when he wished me good night at the stairs and proceeded to his own room. The next morning I found myself staring in the wardrobe wondering what to expect. I'd shaved my legs and all my other bits, which felt a bit presumptuous, but I couldn't imagine that Holden was going to keep his hands to himself. Not when he had an entire day to do whatever he pleased with me.

A tremble of anticipation rolled through me, and I closed my eyes trying to will it away. It was an entirely inappropriate response. "You're doing this because you don't have a choice," I reminded myself. "You have to look out for your own interests."

But the truth was that I'd laid in bed, heart racing, and pictured all the ways Holden could exact payment for his silence. I'd given myself freely to Spencer. He'd shown me gentle attention and taken me roughly. I wasn't exactly wanting in the sexlife department. But there was something entirely different about what I'd agreed to with Holden.

I'd given him control. I'd agreed to his rules—whatever they might be—and that didn't frighten me, it electrified me.

Despite that I chose the most boring undergarments I'd brought on the trip. Given my decision to wear only sexy lingerie, they were hardly modest. But the nude lace bra and knickers were tame compared to some of the other sets I'd packed. Still, I found myself turning in the full length mirror to assess how I looked.

I stared at the woman reflecting back at me.

"Dirty girl," I accused harshly. She didn't even blink.

Knowing that Holden usually kept things casual, I opted for a pair of loose, faded jeans and a cream-colored, cashmere sweater with a wide neck that hung loosely off one shoulder. I'd long since foregone Kerrigan's habit of picking shoes first. Today, I didn't know what shoes to pick. Would we stay here? Would we leave? I gave up trying to guess and shuffled downstairs in a pair of socks.

I froze on the stairs when I spotted Holden standing in the foyer.

"What?" he called up. "You look like you've seen a ghost."

"I just assumed you would be having breakfast like usual." I shook off my surprise and continued down the staircase.

A slow smile spread across his face as if this somehow pleased him. It widened as he looked me up and down, only falling away when he reached my feet. "You look beautiful, but where are your shoes?"

"Do I need shoes?" I challenged him.

"They're generally recommended for walking."

"So, we're going somewhere." I waited for him to tell me more, but he simply nodded. "Where?"

"It's a surprise," he hedged.

"How will I know what shoes to wear?"

"We're in Yorkshire," he answered in a dry tone, "so skip anything with a heel. Boots or laces, dirty girl."

I heaved a frustrated sigh, hoping I sounded appropriately put out and raced back upstairs. I'd only brought one pair of boots, since Spencer had mentioned the possibility of horseback riding. They were made of buttery leather that rose nearly to my knees. It took me a moment to tug them on. Then, I headed back down to meet Holden.

As soon as we were out the door, he headed toward his SUV.

"So we're driving somewhere?" I asked as he opened the passenger door and held it for me.

"Yes, Nancy Drew. Stop looking for clues and just go with it."

"But—" I started.

He cut me off. "My rules, remember?"

I slouched into the seat, only moving to buckle up when he started the engine. As soon as my belt was fastened, I turned my attention out the window.

"Has anyone ever told you that you're cute when you pout?"

"No shame—"

"My rules." He tskked. "And I say *all* the shameless flirting, especially from *you*."

"You think I'm going to flirt with you?" I laughed.

"I don't think so. I know."

I groaned and twisted as far as I could in the seat. We rode in silence for a few minutes. Finally, Holden cleared his throat.

"You're really going to give me the cold shoulder all day?" he asked.

"Oh, I'm sorry," I said sweetly. "Am I allowed to speak? I wasn't clear on the rules."

"Fine. Tell you what. We have a bit of a drive. On the way home, you can ask me anything you want—within reason—and I'll answer."

"But?" I prompted, knowing there would be a catch.

"I get to ask you anything on the way there."

I pursed my lips as I considered. "Anything?"

"Within reason," he repeated.

I thought about it for a minute before nodding. "Okay. How long are we going to be in the car?"

"About half an hour longer," he said.

"Will you tell me where we're going?"

"Uh-uh," he clucked. "I get to ask the questions on this leg."

"Fine." I crossed my arms over my chest. "What do you want to know?"

"How about something easy? Where are you from?"

"I already told you that." I rolled my eyes. "West Bexby."

"Originally? You grew up there."

"No."

"Where did you grow up, then?" he asked.

"Everywhere."

Holden remained silent and I knew he was waiting for me to give a better answer. "I didn't know my parents, so I kinda bounced around."

"Was there any place memorable?"

I shrugged. "Not really."

I hated talking about myself. There just wasn't much to tell. I hadn't lived the life of luxury that he had. I'd never traveled to exotic locations or gone to fancy schools.

"Favorite food?" he asked.

"Whatever I eat next," I admitted sheepishly.

He glanced over at me, his green eyes sparkling with interest. "Out of curiosity, why?"

"Because there are so many things I haven't tried." I hesitated, feeling the heat of embarrassment climbing up my neck. "And because there were times when I didn't have anything to eat at all."

"Oh." Holden remained quiet for a few minutes as if he hadn't expected my answer. Finally, he cleared his throat and forged on. "You mentioned a flatmate in Pixpy."

"Bexby," I corrected him.

"What's her name?"

"Eliza," I told him. "She's pretty much my only friend."

"Why's that?" Holden merged onto the highway.

"I guess because I moved around so much. Plus, she always made sure bills were paid. She was even the one who convinced me to agree to Tod Belmond's offer."

"How did she do that?" He changed lanes, clearing a

path through the slower vehicles so that he could put his foot on the gas.

"She told me I was crazy if I turned it down."

"Remind me to send her a fruit basket," he said, chuckling.

"Why is that funny?"

"It's just hard to imagine anyone convincing you to do anything."

"You did," I pointed out.

"Don't confuse blackmail with persuasion," he advised me.

"At least, you know you're blackmailing me."

Holden was quiet for a moment, when he finally spoke, his voice was soft. "I know I'm the villain of your story."

"You don't have to be," I whispered.

"Someone has to be." He smirked, but it felt wrong. Forced. He was putting on a show for me. But why? Before I could suss out what he was up to, he asked his next question, "If you could be anything, what would it be?"

"A painter." The answer slipped easily from my mouth, which hung open on my answer.

"Really?" His reaction mirrored mine.

"I mean, if I could be anything," I fumbled for a reason that even I didn't know. "Yeah. I guess so."

"You sound surprised," he pointed out.

"I don't think I've ever really thought about it. I haven't had the luxury," I admitted.

"So, you paint?" He sounded more interested than in any of my answers so far. I'd forgotten that he'd told me once he liked books and art.

"Not really." Now I felt a little stupid. He actually knew about art. I was only a pretender. "I've never had money for things like art supplies. I just like to doodle."

"Then why a painter?" he pressed.

I thought of the framed art hanging on the walls of Hensley and Harewood. "When I see a painting, it makes me feel alive. It's like seeing the world through someone else's eyes."

"Interesting," he said as he exited the highway. I caught a glimpse of a sign for the village of Haworth.

"Why is that interesting?" I asked as I studied the passing countryside for clues as to where we were headed.

"Isn't that what you're doing now? Seeing the world through someone else's eyes?"

I'd never thought about it that way before.

"You should take a painting class," he continued, "with all the money Tod Belmond is going to give you."

A grin tugged at my lips as I realized that I could do that. I could travel. I could go to museums. The whole world would be within reach and I could finally leave the past behind me.

"Last question," he said.

"Are we there?" I peeked out the window but we were still zipping along too fast to make out much.

"Nearly," he confirmed. "Why did you do it?"

"Ten million pounds," I answered promptly.

Holden whistled, his eyebrows jumping with surprise. "I can't say I blame you for that. But that's not an answer."

"I'm pretty sure that I did it because of the ten million pounds," I said dryly.

"You're doing it for that, but why? What will ten million pounds do?"

"Spoken like a rich man," I grumbled. "Do I need a reason other than security? I mean, who in their right mind would turn down that much money?"

"You have a point."

"And," I continued, "I can do whatever I want—be whoever I want. All for the low, low price of one year of my life."

"One year. Ten million pounds," he said as if turning over the idea in his brain.

"And a chance to be free," I added softly.

He nodded as if that much he understood.

Holden pulled into a car park and turned off the engine. I looked around, finally spotting a sign that simply said 'museum.' There were no other clues to where we might be, save for a small stream of people, many wearing cameras around their necks, walking toward a nearby stone building.

"Well?" he prompted.

I turned an embarrassed smile on him and shrugged. "Where are we?"

"Seriously?" he asked. "You couldn't come all the way to Yorkshire and not see where the Brontës lived."

I bit back a smile, and he glared at me.

"Out with it, dirty girl."

"You are secretly a nerd," I told him.

"No, I am proudly a very hot nerd," he corrected me. He flashed me a smile that threatened to melt my knickers as he got out of the car.

I was halfway out when he appeared at the passenger door. "You're making me look bad."

"Don't start pretending to be a gentleman now," I advised him.

"I'm always a gentleman. I pride myself on ladies coming first," he said with a wink that left no room for misinterpretation.

"Shameless," I muttered, brushing past him and continuing on toward the building.

Holden caught up with me in two large strides and offered me his arm. I opened my mouth to protest, but he shot me a warning look. His rules. I sighed and wedged my arm through his. We continued on, Holden pointing out small items of interest as we made our way inside.

"So you've been here before?" It was hardly a gamble on my part, given Holden's evident wealth of knowledge.

"I come here every time I'm in Yorkshire. I must have been here twenty-five times, at least." He glanced over at me, his eyes sheepish. I found myself staring not at the brutal, sensual man who seemed intent on destroying everything including himself, but someone charming, boyish even. His sharp, wicked edges softened with each step we took inside the house.

I'd never been particularly interested in classic novels, but I found myself hanging onto every word he spoke as he shared anecdotes and memories from his previous visits. Something about his passion inflamed my own.

"You really love them," I said thoughtfully as he showed me to the back of the house.

"They wanted so much more than their short, tragic

lives gave them," he said as we stepped outside to a breath-taking view of the moors. The wind blew fiercely around us, sweeping his hair across his forehead. It caught mine, tossing it all around my face. Holden reached out and brushed it from my eyes, his fingers drifting down to my cheek. Our eyes locked. "A bunch of parson's daughters and they gave us some of the greatest books of all time. They were fearless."

"I wish I were fearless," I murmured, gazing up at him.

He brushed his thumb over my lower lip. "So do I."

Another gust sent my hair flying again, breaking the spell. I pulled away, turning my attention back to the moors. I stared at their bleak beauty and understood why the authors had felt so inspired. "I wish I could paint these."

"Settle for drawing?" he asked, removing a sketchbook from his pocket.

"You carry a sketchbook?" I asked in surprise.

"I still draw," he said nonchalantly.

"Do you write?"

His expression darkened. A moment passed and he shook his head. "Not for a long time."

The sadness in his voice made my heart ache. I didn't dare ask him why he'd given it up. It was evident that something had forced his hand. But I couldn't stand to see him so melancholy.

"I'll make you a deal," I said.

"You will? I thought we were playing by my rules today."

"Hear me out. I'll sketch." I paused and took out my

mobile. Swiping its screen, I found the app I was looking for. "But you have to write something."

"On your phone?"

"Write something for me, and I'll draw something for you in your book," I said.

His eyes narrowed but finally he tilted his head in agreement. "You are very persuasive."

"And I don't even need blackmail to convince you," I said sweetly.

He grabbed my phone and handed me the sketchbook, barely hiding a wry smile. "One hour. Meet back here."

The moors drew me away from the building, and I found myself walking toward the desolate landscape that seemed to stretch on forever. Finally I stopped and sank onto the earth. For a moment, I stared out wondering what there was to sketch. If I could paint, I would try to capture the colors: the muted grey-blue sky, the silver clouds that hung so low I felt sure I could touch them if I walked farther, and the thick, wild grass that had taken on its funeral shroud early, dying slowly as winter neared. But all I had was the sketchbook and a bit of charcoal tucked inside it.

I touched it to the paper and my hands began to move, almost as if I'd been possessed. I didn't stop. I went through page after page, trying to capture the tiniest details around me, until a shadow fell over me. I looked up, blinking, to find Holden watching over my shoulder.

"That's brilliant," he murmured.

I looked at my watch and gasped. "I'm so sorry!"

Nearly two hours had passed since we'd parted near the parsonage.

"Don't be. I've been watching you for an hour," he admitted.

"Why didn't you interrupt?" I started up and Holden bent to help me. When I was on my feet, I brushed off bits of earth from my jeans.

"I couldn't bring myself to stop you. You looked so...happy."

I smiled, looking to the spot of flattened grass from where I'd been sitting. "I was."

"You should draw more." he took the sketchbook and flipped through the pages. I found myself looking over his shoulder. I'd barely been aware of what I was doing in the moment. I was surprised at what I saw now.

I'd drawn the moors and the clouds, focusing each sketch on some minute detail: a tree in the distance, a rocky crag jutting from the earth, a patch of lingering heather that refused to yield its summer beauty. The rest of each picture consisted of harsh, bold lines drawn with a confidence I couldn't quite explain.

"I see why you love coming here," I told him. "It's inspiring."

Holden's throat slid as he studied me for a moment. His eyes undressed me, took me apart, devoured me. Finally, he tore his gaze away. "We should go. You must be hungry."

He turned and strode away, leaving me to feel naked and vulnerable in the piercing winds of Yorkshire.

19

———————

Today was nothing like I expected. After our visit to the parsonage, we had fish and chips in the village. Then, we wandered through, poking our heads into small shops. I'd practically had to drag Holden out of a rare bookshop. As it was, more than a few volumes came with us. By the time, we climbed back inside the Land Rover, I'd completely forgotten that I was here under threat of blackmail. It wasn't until we reached the highway that he cast a furtive look my way.

"Well?" he prompted.

"Hmm?" I murmured, tearing myself away from the views of the moors to turn to him.

"I promised you could ask me anything you wanted on the way home," he said. "Did you forget?"

"Actually, I did." I'd been so caught up in the day's adventure that I hadn't thought of a single question. I frowned. Now that I was on the spot, there were too many questions crowding my brain and vying for attention.

"Don't tell me you don't have anything you want to know." Another glance. This one more worried.

"I have too many questions." I adjusted my seatbelt, which had begun cutting into my neck and shifted so that my body was angled toward his seat. "Tell me about you and Kerrigan."

"That's not a question." He grinned like he knew he was being a total shit.

"What happened between you and Kerrigan?" I asked.

"That's a big question," he said.

I answered with a sugary smile, "Good thing that we have a long car ride."

"Not that long," he muttered. He switched lanes, his eyes scanning the road as if he might find where to begin on the pavement.

"Where did you meet?" That was a simpler question, but one that might help him get started.

"Year eleven," he said, surprising me.

"She was at Woldingham," I said suspiciously.

"One point for Kate," he muttered. "Yes, she was."

"Last I checked, Woldingham was a school for girls."

"Girls are my favorite subject," he teased.

I stared him down, waiting for a real answer.

"I was at Eton. God love the British for sending their children away to school less than an hour's train into the city." he said. "Kerrigan used to ride in for weekends with her girlfriends. Someone's parents are always out of town, so they would just bounce from house to house doing as they pleased."

"And you did the same?" I guessed.

"Whenever I could. Eton is practically in London."

"And your mother didn't know?" I asked.

His head fell back and he laughed. The car drifted toward the other lane and I shrieked just as Holden casually kept control of the wheel. "As soon as we were old enough for boarding school, she shipped us off. We didn't go home except for holidays. Spencer went home when grandfather requested it."

"Some things never change," I said. "He never asked you."

"No." There was a bitter edge to his answer, but he pressed on, "I didn't mind."

"Because you always had somewhere to crash?" That didn't surprise me. Holden could talk his way into Buckingham Palace if he wanted to.

He flashed me a Chesire grin. "Many beds were open to me."

"Like Kerrigan's?" I asked slowly.

But he shook his head. "Never."

"I thought you were in love," I said dramatically.

"We were," he murmured. "That's why I never went to bed with her."

"Wait? You never..."

"We were young. We had time," he said. "It's easy to jump into bed with someone, but Kerrigan wasn't just anyone."

I tilted my head, wishing the light wasn't fading so quickly outside the window. I wanted to see the secrets he kept—the ones he struggled to hide when he spoke of her—better. "What do you mean?"

"She was alive," he said. "Fearless. She lived like she was on borrowed time. We could talk for hours. One time, she got up on a table at a pub and sang God Save the King just to embarrass a friend of hers. She was joy and chaos rolled into the most beautiful woman I've ever seen."

Holden had said he was in love with Kerrigan. He'd used the past tense, but as he spoke I realized he was still in love with her. It was palpable. It made my chest hurt, like my own heart was trying to break free to search for that kind of love.

"But you never slept with her?"

"You're really hung up on that." He gave me a sidelong look. "No. She wanted to wait until we were at university. And I didn't care because kissing her was better than the best sex I've ever had."

"You expect me to believe that?" I laughed.

"It was," he said seriously. "The only regret I have in life is that I'll never kiss her again. Not like that."

Pain echoed in his words, and I believed him.

"What happened?" I asked quietly, starting to feel guilty for asking about something so personal. He'd questioned me about who I was and all I wanted was to dig up dirt. But I had to know if there was a link between their starcrossed romance and her running away.

"An argument. I was being thick. I don't even remember what it was." He shook his head. "It should have blown over, but then she got into Oxford, and Spencer wanted to go to St. Andrew's."

"So you followed your brother instead of the girl." They really did have a complicated relationship. "And Spencer didn't know about you two? He didn't come with you to London on weekends?"

"Not once. I don't know if he was more worried about his grades or getting bad press."

"No seventeen-year-old is worried about bad press," I snorted.

"Spencer was," he said flatly. "He was groomed to care. Everything he did had to be perfect. He had to be at the top of every class. There was no room for failure. We were best friends at school, but we lived two completely different lives outside of it. Fuck, he didn't even lose his virginity until we were at St. Andrew's."

"Why do I suspect you had something to do with that?" I arched an eyebrow.

"In my defense, it was a birthday present," he said, adding a cocky, "for both of us."

"So you were a virgin, too?"

This earned me another laugh. "No."

"And his first time, you and he?"

"Dirty girl," he said in mock outrage, "you're asking very personal questions."

"I was told I could ask you anything." I held up a hand in defense.

"You just seem so interested in hearing stories about the two of us. It might be easier if you just let us show you," he purred.

I squeezed my thighs together, squirming in my seat. Just the insinuation was enough to make me wet. I found myself thankful for the night blanketing us in darkness, because my face felt as hot as my knickers.

"I was just thinking that's where it all began," I said with a casual shrug that didn't match with my rapid pulse. I needed to douse these flames—and quickly. "Besides, Spencer doesn't want to share me."

"Okay," he said, sounding unconvinced.

"And you..." I trailed off. It took me a moment to gather my wits. "You said you wouldn't want to, either."

"I'm not interested in Spencer's hand-me-downs." He practically spit the words. Then clamped his eyes shut. His jaw tightened as he stared into the night ahead.

I sat in complete shock for a moment, searching for the right response. I spit it back at him when I found it, "Fuck you."

I turned in my seat and stared out the window. The night had swallowed the countryside whole. The lights of passing cars blurred as we passed them, the only break in the monotonous void. I couldn't even see the stars. My throat felt raw. When I swallowed, it constricted on the tears trying to work their way to my eyes. But the last thing I would do is let Holden Byrd see me cry.

I'd nearly fallen for his charm this afternoon. I supposed it was a kindness that he'd shown his cruelty before I became a victim of it. But it wasn't the harsh rejection that had hurt, it was watching the man I'd seen glimpses of this afternoon vanish. Where was the Holden that knew an encyclopedia's worth of Brontë sister trivia? Where was the man who carried a sketchbook in his pocket and looked longingly at the moors? How could one person have two such totally different sides?

"You remind me of her." His quiet words shattered the silence, but I didn't look at him. "I think that's why..."

I wanted to press him to finish the sentence, but caring about what Holden thought would only destroy me. I'd gotten off easily. When he'd asked for twenty-four hours, I'd fully expected to spend them in his bed. Somehow that would have been easier. *Transactional*. I'd already sold my virginity to win Spencer in Kerrigan's name. Sleeping with his twin would only ensure my end of the bargain with Tod Belmond. It was harder to like Holden. It was harder to be disappointed in him. It hurt more.

I don't know if five minutes passed or twenty. I couldn't find the right words to respond until the lights of Hensley appeared on the horizon. "I'm *nothing* like her."

Holden didn't respond and the last few minutes stretched like a wire between us being pulled in opposite directions. When we finally pulled into the drive of Hensley House, I wanted to run inside and lock the door behind me. But I'd made a deal with him. I glanced at the clock and sighed with relief.

"Five more minutes," I warned him, and then we could stop pretending to be civil to one another. "Want to get in a few final shots?"

Holden's head fell and he exhaled. He turned to face me with a tight smile. "I'm sorry."

"Whatever." I already had one hand on the door handle. If we drew this out, I'd be free of him by the time we got inside.

"No, really," he said firmly. His hand reached for mine, and I resisted the urge to draw mine away. I regretted it the instant our skin touched. A burst of electricity sang through me. I forced myself to stay still, not wanting him to see how it affected me. But even in the dark, Holden's eyes flamed as if he felt it, too. "I'm angry with myself, and I took it out on you and that's not okay."

"How self-aware of you." I shook my hand free. "I'm not just some object for you or your brother to play with!" But wasn't I exactly that? A toy bought for the express purpose of entertaining Spencer Byrd until his investment piece was finished?

"I don't think of you that way."

"You called me a hand-me-down," I reminded him, my voice cracking.

"Because..." He took a deep breath and plunged forward, "Because I hate him for having you. I hate that he deserves you like you're some prize."

"Prize?" I repeated in a strangled voice.

"You're misunderstanding me," he said quickly. "I meant that they're giving you to him like that. You are a prize." He looked at my face and backpedaled again. "But definitely not an object or a toy!"

I glared at him in stony silence while he continued to elucidate the ways in which I was both irresistible but not an object until something strange bubbled inside me. Before I could stop it, laughter spilled out of me. Holden paused mid-sentence and stared.

"You...really...did..." I struggled to speak because I was giggling so hard. "...take...Women's Studies."

Holden's shoulders slumped and he shook his head, but

even he began to grin. He glanced at the dash. "One minute and you're free of me."

I took a deep breath, my cheeks hurting from the laughter. "Any last requests?"

"Just one." His body shifted, shortening the distance between us. "I want to kiss you."

"You've kissed me before," I said, trying to act unperturbed as my hands grew slick.

"I want to kiss *you*. Not you pretending to be someone else. You. Not the woman pretending to be engaged to my brother. *You*."

His words stole my breath. I felt pinned to the seat under his heady gaze, and all I could manage was a soft, "Your rules."

Holden brushed the back of his hand down my cheek and cupped my chin. His head angled as he lifted my face to meet his. There was a moment of hesitation that seemed to last an eternity before his mouth crushed softly to mine. There was no urgency or demand. It was as if we'd both traveled a long way and stumbled upon each other somewhere in the middle. There was no rush as my lips parted to his and the kiss deepened. My arms circled his neck and I wove my fingers into his hair, dimly aware that each second brought us closer to farewell. When Holden moved to draw away, I caught his lower lip between my teeth and forced him back to me.

I didn't care if the minute was up along with our excuses. I could only think of him. The energy between us shifted. Holden's hand slipped to the back of my neck and tightened there. My body fought against the seat belt and I dropped a hand trying to find the buckle blindly. Holden found it first and released me. I tried to crawl into his lap, only to be thwarted by the center console.

Holden broke away, breathless, his eyes wild. Before I could stop panting, he was out of the car and around it. The passenger door flew open and he lifted me from the seat. My legs circled his waist as I pressed my needy center against his groin, grinding against his hardening cock. We crashed into one another in a tangle of limbs and tongues.

This is wrong.

And that's what made it so good that it almost felt right. Every inch of me was alive as if Holden had found a secret fuse inside me and lit it. I was on fire and every stolen touch pushed me towards detonation.

I tore my lips away and whispered, "Take me to bed."

Holden's eyes closed and he pressed his forehead to mine. The moment stretched out. I brushed my lips against his, earning me a heavy sigh. A moment later, he placed me on my feet. My fingers caught his shirt and I stared at him, waiting for him to make a move—to explain why he'd stopped. But all he did was lean forward and kiss my head with a quiet "goodbye" before he turned and disappeared into the night.

20

I didn't see Holden the following day. I waited for him to find me and explain, but the more time passed, the more relieved I was that he'd walked away. My life was complicated enough without adding one more mistake to my list. And that's what sleeping with Holden would have been. At least, that's what I told myself.

Hensley felt more like a prison than a refuge now. I'd had no word from Spencer and more than once I found myself staring at the keys to the McLaren, wondering if I should just drive back to London and leave this place behind.

"If Holden would even let me," I grumbled to myself. He would be livid if he found out I took the car from Yorkshire to London, which actually made the idea more appealing. I groaned and threw the book I'd been trying to read for an hour across the bed. "Stop poking the bear!"

That's exactly what I was doing after all. I'd been testing Holden to see how he would respond, and it had nearly cost me. How much was I willing to lose before I learned my lesson? There had to have been a reason that Kerrigan had ended things with him. Probably a dozen judging from his mercurial personality.

By the time the sun set, I was done trying to entertain myself. Crawling into bed, I burrowed under the linens and fell into a fitful sleep. But my problems followed me. In my dreams, both Spencer and Holden waited for me. I found myself in Spencer's arms only to discover I'd actually been kissing Holden. I only understood in that way dreamers do that it wasn't the same man but the brothers shifting into one another and then back again. But in my sleep, both could give me pleasure without consequence and I found my body pinned beneath their hands and tongues. I writhed under Holden's mouth, feeling my body mounting toward release. Closer. Closer.

"Dirty girl."

"Kerrigan."

They was both here and I gave in to it as I climbed and climbed.

A kiss brushed my mouth and I startled awake. Holden's face came into view, hovering over mine with a sly smile. "You were moaning in your sleep."

I moaned again, hooking an arm around his neck and dragging him towards me. He hadn't been able to resist. He wanted me as badly as I wanted him. "You came anyway."

"I told you I would." He nibbled my neck, his body moving between my welcoming legs. "I'm sorry it took so long."

"You're here," I murmured as my hands slipped under his shirt.

"I wish I'd never left." He buried his face into my neck, nipping it between his teeth. "I'd much rather be here than bloody Parliament."

My eyes snapped open, staring at the bed's canopy as I awakened fully.

Spencer.

Spencer was back.

Spencer was in bed with me.

A pang of disappointment shot through me and I moved my head to find Spencer's mouth. I kissed him to chase it away and remind myself that I'd chosen him.

A rough hand pushed between our bodies, slipping between my legs to push my knickers aside. Spencer groaned. "You're so fucking wet. Christ, were you dreaming about me?"

I evaded the question with another kiss, which seemed to satisfy him.

Spencer pushed a finger inside me and began to pump leisurely. "I've been thinking."

"Hmmm?" Conscious thoughts started to fade as I lost myself to the sensations building where he touched me. He was the one who made me feel this way. I'd forgotten. I'd been duped by Holden's identical face and coy charm.

"I think..." He nuzzled my ear, his breath tickling its shell. "...that we should invite Holden to join us."

I slammed a hand into his chest and pushed him off me. Pushing up, I grabbed a pillow and clutched it. "What? No!"

"Kerrigan," he said calmly, giving me a reassuring smile. "I saw how you watched him the other night, and you got so excited that night that we—"

"I don't think it's a good idea," I cut him off. "He flirts with me enough."

But Spencer only rolled his eyes. "And once he's had you, he'll get bored and move on. Although, if you like it, I'm sure that we can arrange..." He walked his fingers along my thigh and turned a knowing smirk on me. "Just imagine both of us inside you."

I had. Repeatedly. I wasn't about to admit that to him, though.

"We're getting married," I said slowly. "I'm going to be your wife. Do you really want to share me with your brother?"

"I share everything with him. I always have—even the womb," he said casually. Spencer reached for the pillow and tossed it to the side.

"What are you doing?" I asked as he lowered his head between my legs.

"A demonstration." He pressed his lips to my slick sex. Just the light kiss sent me reeling. "Imagine my mouth on you while he fucks you."

"Why would I—?"

His tongue dipped lower, parting me so that he could close his lips over my clit's already ragged bundle of nerves. My objection vanished as he sucked harder. Then he was gone. I cried out in frustration and he laughed.

"Imagine that with my cock inside you," he coaxed.

"I thought it was your mouth," I said breathlessly.

"My cock. His mouth. Vice versa. We're identical, remember?"

His words rocketed through me and landed in my core, nearly sending me over the edge.

"Or," he continued as he dropped a featherlight kiss on my thigh, "we could both be inside you. One here and one —" he bent lower and flickered his tongue over a more forbidden place "—here."

The dark touch alone sent my body shaking.

"Just think about it, okay?"

I nodded, my hand catching the front of his shirt and wrenching him to me. "Now would you stop talking and fuck me."

His mouth carved into the crooked grin I was growing to love. "It would be my pleasure."

21

The bed was empty the next morning. I stretched my arm across the imprint Spencer had left in the sheets and found his place cold. For a crazy moment, I wondered if I'd dreamed the whole thing. I sat up and looked around the room. My gaze landed on a pair of polished Berlutis and I relaxed. He was here. He was real.

Almost instantly my relief turned to dread, churning in my stomach like sludge. If he was really here then he'd really tried to talk me into a threesome with Holden last night. My core clenched as if to send its opinion on the matter. I threw myself back in bed, grabbed a pillow, and smothered a scream with it. How had everything become this screwed up?

After a few minutes, I pried myself from the warm bed. I lingered in the hot shower, hoping the water might clear my head. But when I finally turned off the faucet, I still felt as foggy as the air hanging in the steamy room. I dressed quickly, eager to get this morning's awkward breakfast out of the way.

Twelve hours ago I'd kissed Holden and asked him to take me to bed.

Eight hours ago, I'd screwed Spencer senseless trying to sate myself.

Why not have scones with the both of them to remind myself of the utter clusterfuck I'd found myself in?

But when I dragged myself onto the veranda, I found Spencer sitting alone with a copy of *The Guardian* and a cup of tea. He tipped his head without looking over at me as he continued to read. "Good morning."

I chewed my lip as I took the seat next to his. The morning air nipped at my skin and I scooted my chair closer to the gas heater someone had thoughtfully placed by the table. This morning's spread was sparse compared to what I'd grown accustomed to at Hensley. I half-heartedly took an egg and topped it.

One of the kitchen staff appeared to bring a fresh pot of hot water.

I smiled up at him. "Could I trouble you for some toast?"

"Of course," he said brightly. "Will you need anything else?"

"That's all," Spencer answered for me. He folded the newspaper and placed it on the table. "It's my fault. I told them a light breakfast. Holden always orders like it's a Roman orgy. I'm sure you've had more scones than any woman in England this week."

My smile drooped. "Well, I love scones, so it was no hardship."

"Who doesn't? But probably best to moderate considering," he said as he picked up his phone.

"Considering?" I repeated.

"With the wedding. Don't brides go on crazy diets?"

I swallowed the bite of egg I'd just taken. It slid uneasily down my throat. "I suppose."

"Sorry," he said swiftly, looking up from his mobile to find me frowning at him, "I didn't mean to offend you. That was a stupid thing to say."

"It's fine," I said mildly, and we both fell silent. "How are things in London? Your grandfather?"

"He'll outlive us all," he predicted as a plate of toast was laid on the table before us. He looked up at the man who'd delivered it. "Scones please."

At least, he wasn't going to force me into some diet.

"I hope Holden didn't bother you too much," Spencer said as I nibbled on my toast.

"No. We even drove into Haworth together." It was only partially true. Holden hadn't bothered me in the way that Spencer meant, but he had gotten under my skin.

Spencer groaned and rolled his eyes. "He took you to Jane Austen's home? I'm sorry."

"It was the Brontë's home, actually," I corrected him. "And I enjoyed it, especially the moors."

"You sound as hopelessly romantic as he is."

"Hopelessly romantic? Holden?" I cocked an eyebrow at Spencer. "Are we talking about the same person?"

"Romantic in the way he sees the world. The sky isn't

cloudy, it's shadowed," Spencer mocked. "Do yourself a favor and never go to a museum with him. He never shuts up."

"Noted." The platter of scones arrived. I picked one up and took a bite. It crumbled, dry and flavorless, on my tongue.

"We'll do something fun today, I promise," he continued, taking a sip of his tea.

"We had plenty of fun while you were gone," Holden announced as he joined us on the veranda. He pulled out a chair and sat across the table from me. "Didn't we, dirty girl?"

Spencer's bemused grin fell from his face. "As charming as the anecdote behind that pet name is, I think it's best that you stop using it. We wouldn't want others to ask, would we, darling?"

He was looking at his brother, but it was clear he was speaking to me. I stared between them, but neither indicated I was there. They were locked in an aggressive stare. I had to make a choice. Spencer was drawing a line and asking me to step to one side.

But he also wanted them to take me to bed—together.

There was no reason behind any of it. I was expected to act one way in public and behave another way in private. I needed to be the portrait of the perfect fiancée on his arm and his willing whore in the bedroom. A week ago, I'd been fine with that arrangement.

Because a week ago, I thought it was my choice.

Suddenly, I wasn't so certain.

"If it bothers you, ask him to stop," I finally said.

"It doesn't bother you?" Spencer pressed, his eyes still glued to his brother.

It did. I had asked Holden to stop. But something about Spencer's demeanor kept me from admitting that.

"You two can sort this out," I said. Both their heads swiveled to me. Spencer looked shocked. Holden smirked. "Keep me out of your pissing contests."

Because that's what this was—a pissing contest—and I was the ultimate prize.

"Fine," Spencer said in a clipped tone, redirecting his attention to his brother. "I'll make you a deal. Stop calling her that, stop flirting with her, give up this fascination you've developed to get back at me, and I'll give you what you really want."

I gasped, but neither of them seemed to notice. I might be the prize, but this wasn't about me.

A muscle ticked in Holden's jaw. He sat rigidly in the chair and glared at him. "And what is that, brother?"

"One night," he said simply, and my body went cold. "I'll give you one night with her."

Holden glanced at me, his lips smashed into a thin line as if he didn't dare to speak.

"Spencer," I murmured, doing my best to restrain myself. This had to be a joke, or, at the very least, his way of proposing a threesome like he'd done last night. "I don't—"

"Shhh," Spencer hushed me. "He's thinking."

I froze, not because I didn't know what to say but because I didn't know what to lob at him first. Feelings crowded my brain, stampeding toward my mouth, and I tried to sort through them to find the most hurtful thing I could. Because I needed to get his attention. I needed to draw my own line. I should have done so much sooner than this moment.

"With you?" Holden finally asked through gritted teeth. His gaze darted at me as if warning me to stay silent.

"If you want," Spencer continued. "Or you can have her all to yourself." His mobile vibrated on the table. He lifted and frowned when he saw the screen. "Excuse me, a moment. I need to take this."

He stood and answered. I sat in stunned silence watching him take the stairs that led from the stone veranda to the gardens below. He was too far away to hear what call was so important that he'd interrupted his own sales pitch.

My lashes grew heavy and hot, and I blinked with confusion, surprised when tears ran down my cheeks.

"Are you..." Holden trailed off. A moment later his fist slammed into the tabletop with a crack. A crack splintered across it and I pushed away afraid the glass would shatter. It held, but it was permanently ruined. "Fuck. Of course, you aren't okay. Fuck him."

"Maybe, he just..." I mumbled as I searched for a reason.

"No. Don't make excuses for him," Holden demanded.

"He told me that he'd never have to force me." I sniffed, swiping at my tears. I was such an idiot. "He told me I'd always do what he wanted because that's what I would want. I thought he respected me. But I was just a gift for him to do with as he pleased."

"You aren't an object," Holden interjected. "You're—"

"I am," I stopped him. "Tod Belmond bought me—

body, soul, and virginity to boot—and gave me to him. I belong to Spencer until Kerrigan comes back or this year is up." I swallowed and forced a smile. "I'm sorry."

"What on earth are you apologizing to me for?" he asked, still trembling with barely suppressed anger.

"It wouldn't be that bad to spend a night with you," I said quietly. "Actually, it wouldn't be bad at all. I mean, I tried to get you into bed yesterday." I tried to smile but found that I couldn't. I felt too heavy to carry even a sign of happiness.

"It would be that bad," Holden said with disgust. "So let me make this clear. I will never lay another finger on you..."

"Holden!" I choked on his name as he stood and glowered over me.

"...unless you ask me to," he finished, sweeping away my objections. Wordlessly, he left without so much as a glance toward the gardens his brother paced in.

Spencer's call continued after he'd gone, and with each second that ticked by I bolstered myself to face him. When he finally mounted the stairs and started toward me, I knew exactly what I wanted—no *needed*—to say to him. The words were poised on the tip of my tongue when I spotted the slump of his shoulders. I hesitated, realizing his eyes followed his feet as his head hung down. When he finally lifted his face to mine, the anguish there changed everything.

"Spencer?" I called in concern.

"It's my grandfather," he said in a hollow voice. "He's dead."

22

I'd barely processed this when Spencer's grief seemed to snap in two. Behind it, he wore a mask of determined resilience. "I need to make a few calls before we leave."

"I can pack," I offered, switching directions as quickly as my brain would allow.

"Thank you," he said as he lifted his mobile to his ear. "And tell Holden."

I started, popping up from my chair to object, but he was already speaking to someone on the other line. Pinning my arms to my sides, I marched inside, determined to get it over with. It hadn't been an order, I told myself, but a request. There had to be a million things to take care of. Spencer had to delegate.

That didn't make climbing the stairs any easier. I'd reached the second floor when I realized that I had no clue which room was his. I paused, wishing someone would come along to point me in the right direction. But life never worked that conveniently. Life didn't come with pre-programmed navigation. Finally, I took a deep breath and started walking.

A door flew open so hard that it slammed into the wall, and I froze in place. A moment later, Holden appeared with a suede duffle. He halted when he saw me standing there.

"I'm leaving," he told me. "It's not...what's wrong?"

I wasn't crying or anything. I hadn't known Lord Byrd well enough to be sad, but my stomach was twisted into knots over delivering the bad news.

"Your grandfather..." How was I supposed to tell him this?

"Did the old goat fall again? Let me guess, you and Spencer must immediately depart so he can lock you back in your cage while he runs his errands." Holden rolled his eyes. He shifted his bag over his shoulder, showcasing the flex of his muscles.

I forced myself to spit the news out. "He's dead."

Holden fell silent. We stood and stared at each other.

"I think I'm supposed to feel something," he said slowly. "Why don't I..."

"Shock," I murmured. "You'll feel sad later."

"Maybe," he said darkly.

"Spencer wants us to leave for London. Arrangements have to be made and—"

"Already on my way," Holden cut me off, lifting the bag slightly as evidence. "Not that he needs me to help with anything."

We both knew Spencer would run the show. It's what

he'd been groomed to do for years. His family had been preparing him for this moment. He would handle everything, but that didn't mean it was going to be easy. "He'll need you."

"He never has before," he said bitterly.

"We both know that's not true." I waited for him to challenge me, but he didn't.

"Look on the bright side, dirty girl," he said, and this time I found the nickname welcome and familiar, "you'll be rid of me soon."

"What if I don't want to be rid of you?" I blurted out.

"You're going to be a Duchess, mistress of Sparrow Court. You won't want me hanging around," he said with quiet finality.

"That doesn't mean we can't—"

"This changes everything. Especially us." He stepped toward me, close enough that we could reach for each other but far enough that we didn't touch. "I could never settle for a scrap of you. I want all of you. I always will."

"You barely know me," I breathed.

Holden loosed a hollow laugh. "I know you better than you know yourself."

"So that's it," I challenged him. "You're just going to say that and walk away. What about Kerrigan? Now you're over her?"

"I never said that."

"I wouldn't settle, either. For part of you," I nearly choked on the words.

"You wouldn't have to."

"And when Kerrigan comes back? What about then?" I

pressed. "Spencer wants her pedigree. You want her love. There's no room for me."

"Kerrigan's not coming back, and even if she did...she wouldn't be my Kerrigan anymore."

A chill chased away my anger. It darted up my back and settled at the nape of my neck. "What do you mean?"

"You know."

"No, I don't." He had no way of knowing that, unless...

"Yeah. You do." He leaned down, angling his face over mine and swept a soft kiss over my mouth. It was so chaste but my lips burned in its wake. "I'll be seeing you, dirty girl."

I stood there long after he left, trying to find a lie to believe in, but all I could swallow was the truth.

23

———

We rode in complete silence. The only debate had been whether we should leave the cars and take a helicopter, or drive. In the end, practicality had won out. Spencer needed to make arrangements, which was easier if he had his own car. It had made for a rather somber return trip.

Despite our trip being cut short, in our absence autumn had officially arrived in London. October was only a few days away with November and December on her heels. I didn't have the stomach to ask Spencer about the wedding. It felt wholly inappropriate to worry about that with a death in the family. But that didn't mean I could stop thinking about it.

When we'd left for Yorkshire, I'd hoped to return with a clear head and the courage to confront Tod Belmond about the change in our arrangement. Today, I felt more muddled than ever, but one thing was apparent: I needed to stop this before it went any further.

I couldn't marry Spencer in Kerrigan's name.

I wouldn't.

Kerrigan had to come home. I didn't care what Holden thought about it. The idea of her returning was like a knife piercing my heart. He didn't think she would come, but when she did would he still look at me like he had in the hallway? Would he still want all of me?

Did I have any of me to even give?

And none of that mattered until the dark days ahead of us were passed. I would stay by Spencer's side while he grieved. I couldn't complicate his life more by forcing the issue of postponing our wedding. Not when part of me was wondering if the whole thing needed to be called off. Taking that time was what he needed, but it would also give me a chance to track down Kerrigan myself. I'd trusted Tod and Giles to handle it. Maybe I had to be the one to show her it was time to return.

We bypassed the heaviest traffic and headed straight to Hampstead. When the car turned down the lane to Willoughby Place, I looked at him in surprise. "Don't you want me to stay with you?"

"I do." He pulled into the drive, stopping at the closed gates. "It's going to be a long night, though, and mother will be there—and Holden and Evie. I just thought you might want a moment to catch your breath."

"Don't worry about me. Let me know what you need," I encouraged him, meaning it completely. I was still angry with Spencer. That had not changed. But this was about more than him. I needed to be there for Evie and Holden, as well.

"I'm sure mother will be furious if you aren't there," he said. "She's already worried about the wedding."

"The wedding can wait," I said, relieved to finally speak the words. "There's no rush—"

Spencer cut me off with a laugh. "We'll be lucky to talk her into waiting until December. She'll want it done before I'm summoned to my grandfather's seat."

"When will that be?" I asked slowly.

"That will depend on the King." He leaned over and kissed me. "It might not be the fairytale you dreamed of, but I'll make it up to you."

Before I could think of what to say, the gate opened. Spencer drove forward, pulling to the entrance. "I can pick you up later. Just call me."

"I can drive," I said, forcing the words over a dry tongue.

"And Kerrigan..." he hesitated. "I'm sorry about earlier when I told Holden he could...I was calling his bluff, but then everything happened." His eyes searched my face. "I didn't want you to think I would have really made that deal. It was incredibly poor timing."

My lips flattened into a line, and I nodded. The movement of my head sent black swirling at the edges of my vision. I dug my fingers into the console between us, determined to keep control. "I knew that."

"Good." He sighed with relief as he wrapped a hand around the back of my neck and drew me closer. "I don't want him to touch you...unless I'm there to enjoy it."

He stroked a thumb across my cheek, drinking me in, and I drowned in his gaze. My head started to swim and I tugged gently away. "You should get going. I'll see you later."

"I'll miss you the whole time," he promised as I climbed out of the car. I didn't bother with my overnight bag. I didn't have time to grab anything but my purse. Everything was getting cloudy, each step I took felt as if I was fighting against quicksand.

The McLaren peeled away before I'd reached the house, and as soon as he was out of sight, I collapsed against the door, clinging to the knob to stay upright. It swung open and I nearly lost my balance.

"I'm sorry," Iris called cheerfully, lunging to stop me from falling to my knees. "I should have looked out the peephole before I opened the door."

"I need to sit down," I told her, locking my legs to stay upright, before bending my knee to take a tentative step.

"Oh darling, it's been a terrible day." She put her arm around my shoulder sympathetically. "We heard the news. Your father is stuck in the city, but I already called and spoke with Caroline on the phone. She sounds devastated. You must be overwhelmed, but I think I have something to cheer you up. Let's go up to your bedroom."

I nodded. With her help I was pretty sure I could stay on my feet. The steadiness of her embrace made it easier to focus on my own breathing. By the time we'd taken the lift up—at her insistence—the attack was already becoming a memory.

"Did you have a lovely time before..?"

"Yes," I lied. Lovely wasn't the word I would choose for any of it. Shakespearean, maybe. Weird. Those seemed like better choices. "I just want to take a nap. Can the surprise wait for tomorrow?"

Iris paused at the door, an apologetic grin on her face. "I'm afraid it can't, but I don't think you'll mind."

She opened the door and proved her point, because a friendly face was waiting for me on the sitting room couch.

Eliza.

24

"I'll leave you two to catch up." Iris patted my shoulder and disappeared down the hall toward her own room.

I took a step inside, slammed the door behind me, and stared, open-mouthed. A second later, Eliza flew at me and hugged me, sending us both into pits of laughter. When we finally calmed down and collapsed onto the sofa, she elbowed me in the ribs.

"I feel like I should curtsy to you or something," she teased. "This place is wild." She held up her arm to reveal a diamond studded Omega wristwatch. "They just let me hang out here. I stole this watch. I hope you don't mind."

"I think Kerrigan Belmond has a watch for every day of the year, it's fine," I assured her.

"We should play dress up," Eliza said wickedly. Before I could protest, she was up, grabbing my arm and dragging me into the closet. We spent the next half an hour concocted the most ridiculous ensembles we could, giggling and teasing each other the whole time. Finally, we collapsed onto the ground. Me in a bundle of fur and her in a mass of tulle and caught our breath.

"I hear you were in the country," Eliza said in a snobbish voice, lifting her nose in the air. "Did you go hunting?"

"I wish. It would have been less bloody," I said with a grim smile. "I was supposed to go with Spencer but Holden showed up."

"Poor Kate. Stuck with two handsome men." She pressed a hand to her forehead. "Whatever did you do with them?"

"Not that," I said dryly, adding a sly, "Not really, at least."

"Ohhh, kinky!" Her eyes sparkled as brightly as the diamond necklace she wore around her neck. "Tea. Spill. Now."

I filled her in on the time I'd spent at Hensley, leaving out the bits about Holden's blackmail.

"You just went with him on a day trip?" She rolled her eyes. "Tell me again that nothing's going on with you two."

I tried to shake my head and failed, earning me a shriek.

"I knew it!" She pointed at me, cackling with unrepentant laughter.

"It's complicated."

"That's a Facebook status, babe," she advised me. "Not how you feel."

"Trust me, it's both." How could I explain all the conflicting emotions warring inside me? And why would I want to when it all came down to one thing? "Neither of them are mine. They never will be. I'm just having fun."

Eliza studied me for a moment, remaining unusually quiet. "That sounds like the kind of fun that's going to get you hurt."

"Yeah." I swallowed but a lump remained lodged in my throat. "But it's the kind of fun that will get me ten million pounds and that will get me any fun that I want."

"So, you're going through with it?" she asked. "I wondered after..."

I arched an eyebrow.

"You sounded upset in the message you left me. I tried to reach you but I kept getting a number-not-in-service notification," she told me.

"That's weird. It was probably the country. There's nothing out there but sheep, grass, and homes filled with billions of dollars in artwork," I said with a shrug. "You didn't have to come all the way to London."

"Like hell I didn't, and besides, this is worth it!" She fluffed the tulle of her ballgown.

"I don't know if I'm going to go through with it," I returned to her earlier question. "I agreed to a year. That was supposed to give Tod time to find Kerrigan and coax her home. Now they want me to get married like yesterday and just use her name—and that feels..."

"Wrong?" Eliza finished for me.

I nodded and lowered my voice. "Not just because it's her life, but because I'm worried about her."

"Do you think something happened to her?" Eliza whispered, scooting closer to me on the ground. It wasn't a stretch to imagine that the walls had ears at Willoughby

Place, but I still felt a little silly sitting in another woman's clothes and whispering in her closet.

"I'm not sure," I admitted. "What if Tod is keeping her away? What if his whole plan is for me to marry Spencer and make it official because she refused?"

"Where would he be keeping her?" Eliza asked uneasily, looking around the closet like she might discover a trapdoor or a secret room.

"I don't know. I found some of her things in his office."

"Okay." She held up her hand. "Hear me out. What if you just ask him?"

"Oh that would be lovely," I said. "Hello, Mr. Belmond, do you have your daughter locked in a dungeon somewhere?"

Eliza stuck out her tongue. "You can be more tactful than that."

"Or..." My mouth widened into a bright smile.

She grimaced, her eyes closing. "I don't like the way you're looking at me."

"It will be easy," I promised her. "I just need a distraction, so I can poke around."

"And I get to be the distraction?" she asked with a sigh. She reached up and took off the diamond necklace. Playtime was officially over.

25

Any guilt I felt about tricking Iris was mitigated when she launched into plans to move the wedding timetable up—over drinks with Eliza. We were seated around a small table in the morning room, Iris's private office in the house, and enjoying a bottle of Chateau Sainte Claire, when she dropped the news that Caroline had already brought it up.

"Spencer mentioned it," I said glumly.

"I'm so sorry this is happening to you," Iris told me, pouring a bit more wine into my glass. "It's still going to be a dream wedding. I'll call the shop tomorrow and demand they rush your dress."

I forced a smile, my fingers clutching my wine glass. I loved Iris for worrying about my happiness. She was possibly the only person in Kerrigan's life that cared. Nausea twisted my stomach as I considered how betrayed she would feel when I found Kerrigan and convinced her to come home. I'd built a relationship with her stepmother despite all evidence that Kerrigan herself hated the woman.

And how would Iris feel about me when she learned the truth?

I'd probably never see her again.

The sad thought left me lingering at the table despite the plan I'd concocted with Eliza earlier.

"You could wear a burlap bag down the aisle and look gorgeous," Eliza said reassuringly.

"She's right." Iris's laugh rang out like a bell. "But I promise it won't come to that." She lounged back, draping a dark arm elegantly over her chair. "So where did you two meet?"

"Oh." Eliza looked at me, her eyes wide. "Well, it was…"

"Bandol," I said quickly, grateful that I'd studied all the maps of Southern France Giles had given me to brush up on. "It's this little town on the Côte d'Azur. Eliza was back-packing."

"And Kerrigan was staying in that ritzy resort. What was it called?" She wiggled her eyebrows over the rim of her glass.

I was going to kill her later. But I'd chosen Bandol, because I actually remembered it. "The one on the private island? It was so lovely. Anyway, we hit it off and then we traveled together for a bit."

"Leaving a string of broken hearts in our wake," Eliza added with a grin.

"I'm sure you did." Iris sighed. "It sounds lovely. I wish I could get your father to take a real honeymoon."

"You didn't go on a honeymoon?" Eliza asked.

"We did, but it was cut short when…" Iris trailed off, but her eyes darted toward me.

"It's my fault," I guessed. "I'm so sorry that I made you all worry."

Kerrigan had disappeared and Tod had come home to find her.

"It all worked out," Iris said brightly, "and, trust me, if that man doesn't take me to Bandol, I'll take myself."

We all laughed appreciatively.

"So, what are you doing now, Eliza?"

Her eyes skipped to me, but she shrugged. "Working in a pub, figuring things out."

"Exactly what you should be doing," Iris said without an ounce of superiority. Of course, she wasn't the type to judge a working woman. She hadn't been born to this extravagance. She knew what the real world was like.

Still, as I watched her chat with Eliza, my chest tightened with jealousy. I wished it was me so at ease with her place in the world. I wished my place in this world didn't have an expiration date. But wishing wouldn't change anything. I placed my wineglass on the table and stood. "Excuse me. I need to run to the loo. Too much wine!"

"There is no such thing," Iris said with a wink as she refilled my glass.

"Iris," Eliza said on cue, "I'm told you're a ballerina…"

The conversation faded as I made my way casually into the hall. I'd been smart enough to keep the key I'd found to Tod's office the first time I'd gone looking for answers. I slipped it out of my pocket, glancing nervously around the hall, and then let myself inside the locked room.

It looked exactly the same as it had last time. Spotless. No sign that a moment of work had been done inside. I went quickly to the corner where I'd found Kerrigan's bag. There was nothing there but shadows. My heart dropped, taking my hopes for answers with it.

"You are such an idiot," I cursed myself. Why hadn't I gone back for it that night? Because I'd been distracted by Spencer and his numerous talents. My weakness would cost me. I didn't have the time to open up books or tear the place apart. Plus, it would be pretty obvious if I ransacked the place. Even worse, I could get someone else in trouble.

I dropped into Tod's chair and stared around the dark study. There was no reason to think there was a shred of information in this room, except for that bloody locked door. Why lock it if there was nothing to hide?

I opened each desk drawer again, finding the same unused office supplies. My fingers paused on the locked drawer. I should have looked for a key or googled how to pick a lock. I pulled the latch with a sigh.

It opened.

I took a deep breath and pulled it the rest of the way from the desk. Inside there was a manilla folder and nothing else. Placing it on the desk, I opened it with trembling fingers. A number of Post-Its had been stuck to one side with meaningless info scrawled across them. One read *Cannes?* Well, that one was easy enough to decipher. Another *New York?* I gulped when I saw *Bexby???* on one.

Had he thought he'd found her only to be disappointed by me?

There were a number of bank statements dating back to Kerrigan's disappearance. My eyes widened when I saw the balance of her bank account. She could be anywhere with that kind of money at her disposal. I flipped through them and noticed something odd.

The balance didn't change.

I paused and studied them more carefully. Kerrigan Belmond hadn't spent a dime of her trust fund since her disappearance. Ice formed in my chest, and I thought of what Holden had said about Kerrigan not coming back. Did he know something he hadn't told me? Something terrible?

Behind the statements there were pictures, and the dread building inside me dissipated a little. It was her. *Alive.* At least, she'd been alive when these pictures were taken. I tried not to think about that untouched bank account. There were a million reasons that she might not need the money. She could have taken cash with her. She might have run off with someone else. Kerrigan had to have tons of rich friends who would foot the bill.

Except, I hadn't met any of them, save for Beatrice and Holden.

I tore through the pictures. There had to be someone else with her. It was the only thing that explained it. I froze when I reached the first picture of me. It had to have been taken before Tod came to find me. But it wasn't the photo those wankers had snapped in the pub. It was like the others: high-quality and professionally shot. It looked like it had been done by a private investigator. There were more. Some of me at the Hare & Hound. Others of me leaving the flat. A few with Eliza. How long had someone watched me before they realized I wasn't Kerrigan Belmond?

Long enough for Kerrigan to slip through their fingers. By the time she had, Tod had no choice but to make his arrangement with me.

But the final sheet in the folder wasn't a folder. I stared at it, reading it over and over, but it didn't make sense. I shoved it to the side. There had to be more. There had to be something that explained all of this. Tod couldn't have given up. No matter what that final report said. Kerrigan was out there, but he'd stopped looking if this file was anything to judge.

"Oh darling!"

My head snapped up to find Iris standing in the doorway, holding a new bottle of wine. She stepped inside and flipped on the light. I stared at her. I wouldn't lie. There was no point. The evidence of what I was doing was strewn across the desk: pictures of her, pictures of me, bank statements. It was all right there in the open. I couldn't hide it with the lights on.

But why was I still in the dark?

"You weren't supposed to see those," she said softly, her shoulders slumping. "Now, there's no choice..."

A sob wrenched from me. I turned, tear-stained eyes on her, realizing only then that I was crying. "What are these?"

"I think we should wait—"

"What are these?" My voice broke on the words.

The door slammed open and Tod stepped in a blustery rage, Eliza peeking around him. I met her eyes, and she looked scared. Tod soaked in the sight before him, the anger radiating from him.

I held up a photo and shook it at him. "Explain this!"

"Goddammit, Kerrigan," he stormed.

"I'm not your daughter," I screamed back at him. "You can't force me to keep pretending that I am! Where is she?" My throat hurt as I collapsed into the seat and cried harder.

"I didn't want to do this," Tod said and I shrank further down. Iris moved quickly, stepping in front of him.

"Think about what you're doing, Tod," she urged him in a desperate murmur. "You know what they—"

"It's over," he said with a note of finality, guiding her gently to the side.

My heart cracked open and I shook my head as he walked to the desk. "Look at me," he said, this time his voice absent of the fury that had yoked him moments ago. Now there was only resignation. "You know where Kerrigan is."

"No." I shook my head.

"You know what happened to her," he continued.

I kept shaking my head until my head began to swim in a sea of starless night. "No!"

"Yes," he said firmly, reaching to grip my wrist, as though he could be my anchor. "You *are* Kerrigan Belmond."

ACKNOWLEDGMENTS

There are so many people to thank that I might miss a few, so if you're reading this: thank you! You're a part of this whether you realize it or not.

Thank you to my agent, Louise Fury, for being a force of nature and to my foreign teams for going above and beyond.

Thank you to my team on the ground. Shelby, you are my eagle eyes and my anchor. Thank you for keeping everything running smoothly when I'm busy in London.

Thank you to the team at Grey's Promotion for being on top of everything and providing another stellar release.

Thank you to my author friends for being a constant, awe-inspiring group of women.

Thank you to my readers, especially my ARC Team! And thanks to Geneva Lee's Loves and all the incredible women who help me keep it fun and sexy in there!

Thanks to Elise for hurting her back, so she could be around to hang while I was writing. Just kidding. Sorta.

Thank you to my family for putting up with deadlines and word lag. I could not do this without your constant understanding and support.

And to Josh, always to Josh. You are my brand of catnip.

ABOUT THE AUTHOR

GENEVA LEE is the *New York Times, USA Today*, and internationally bestselling author of over a dozen novels, including the Royals Saga which has sold two million copies worldwide. She lives in Poulsbo Washington with her husband and three children, and she co-owns Away With Words Bookshop with her sister.

Connect with her online at:
www.GenevaLee.com

Or on social media at:

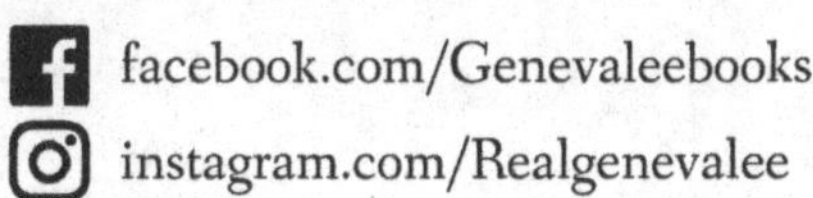

facebook.com/Genevaleebooks

instagram.com/Realgenevalee